Mao's Town

Mao's Town

a Novel

Xie Hong

Hardcover fiction book
ISBN 978-8792632-93-7

Edited: Tui Allen
Published in Denmark by Whyte Tracks Publishing
www.whytetracks-publishing.com

Contents

Chapter 1

They say that horrible childhood experiences will affect the rest of one's life. It is true. I am an example. Now, I hope to find release by sharing those experiences with you, or relating it to the air itself.

I hope it works.

There is an unforgettable picture in my memory. I try hard to get rid of it, but, I fail. Sometimes the cold sweat of my own nightmares drives me back to the old days, back to my hometown in China.

In the nightmare I am surrounded by furious crowds. All around me, people are shouting words that have echoed from my childhood through the rest of my life:

"Take off your clothes!"

"Take off!"

"Take them off!"

But this time, Jing, an excellent tailor in our town, does not follow the order. She wipes tears from her face, glances up to the sky, adjusts her hair and clothes, and walks step by step towards the furnace. She jumps without hesitation, into the flames.

The shouting stops at once. Everything freezes, not only open mouths, but also bodies. Raised hands are lowered slowly. Fists unclench. Everyone is silent. No-one knows what to do. What orders would the officers give now?

"Committed suicide?"

The assembly host Lee, shouts to break the silence.

"This is good for our Revolution!"

Automatically, people mimic his shout, "It is good for the Revolution!"

But this time, their voices fade quickly and the people slip away in silence.

I had seen Red Movies where revolutionaries walked bravely to their own executions, shouting revolutionary slogans. But they were only movies, this was the real world.

A peaceful lady, labeled "spy," has just walked to death by fire in front of me.

Suddenly, a girl named Sun rushes to the furnace, crying aloud.

"Mother! Mother!"

But two women grab her and stop her. Sun struggles and her cries echo to the sky. I run to report to her two sisters and at last, I awake from the nightmare.

I fear those memories, because sometimes they are like a horror movie playing on repeat across my mind. I wanted to know the real reasons for what Jing did that day.

Years later, Sun and I moved overseas from China and we met up again in the United States of America. We tried to keep the old days out of our conversation but in the end we could not avoid talking about it.

Sun was sure that her Mother died for her colorful clothes. Could that be the real answer? I doubted it. But, Sun said that she had thought hard about it.

"...in the end, because she was forced to undress in public, Mother's attitude to clothes changed from love to hate. She had been insulted time and again and gradually she transferred the blame for her shame from herself to the clothes. She jumped into the fire just to punish the clothes - to burn them and cleanse the shame from her body."

Was Sun right to think this way? Why did she choose this answer? At that time I myself had not yet analyzed the events that led to that day. But still, I was uneasy about her conclusion. I suspected she wanted to forget past sorrows and had chosen the most comforting answer.

I knew the real story of her family very well, especially where it concerned her parents, Ahn and Jing, who both died on Mao's stage.

Although Sun and I were so unwilling to touch on those old memories, they were common to us both. We could never stop them from replaying in our brains.

Chapter 2

We were neighbors and Sun was my classmate in primary school. Her family came from overseas and brought many strange and new ideas to our town. They were like our window to the outside world. As a child, I liked to visit the family and every visit refreshed me.

I often played at Sun's house. We sat around the sewing machine. Sun's Mother Jing sewed clothes, telling fairy tales at the same time.

One special thing was the fantastic smell of skin cream that filled the house. It seemed strange that the women in the family used skin cream not only in winter, but also in other seasons.

We children lost ourselves in Jing's fairy tales, imagining that we were characters in the stories. They took us to another world.

Jing never told us where the stories came from. Many years later, I discovered the stories came from Western countries. But only her family knew that, at the time.

They were so different from Chinese traditional folk stories. I learnt so much from them that was fresh and new.

My own parents were too busy to tell me stories. Most of the time they worked away from home, taking part in the denouncement assemblies, writing posters, or criticizing the enemies of Chairman Mao. They seemed as committed as any soldiers fighting in the trenches.

At that time, many high school students joined the Red Guards and became involved in Revolutionary Actions, fighting opponents of the regime. We younger children had nowhere to go, so Sun's home was a wonderful place for us to play.

Among the fairy tales I heard from Jing, were Snow White and The Seven Dwarfs, Thumbelina, The Little Mermaid, and The Princess and the Pea. I specially loved Snow White and The Seven Dwarfs, because Sun and her six pretty sisters, had a number that matched the dwarfs in the story.

We not only listened to the fairy tales, but sometimes also played the story characters in our games. Sun and her six sisters acted as the Seven Dwarfs and I acted as Snow White. I became a girl and they became seven little men. It was all a lot of fun.

I did not tell anyone why I liked to visit Sun's home. It was not only for the fairy tales, but also for those fashion clothes. At that time, all Chinese people dressed in the same dark or grey-coloured clothes, each as gloomy as the other.

Perhaps because I was so young, that gloominess gave me the blues. If others noticed they did not show it because no one dared to discuss it openly. But the monotony depressed me.

The many beautiful clothes in Jing's sewing room created a contrasting world that I hungered for. I did not understand the meaning of fashion. I only knew that the colors, styles and textures charmed my eyes.

I could not tell if the fairy tales were true or false, but I could truly touch the beautiful clothes, and smell the special textiles. I let my fingers skim quietly across the rich fabrics, enjoying their amazing sensations.

One day, I said to Mother, "Chinese New Year is coming up. Can I have new clothes for it?"

Mother smiled and said to me, "I have already prepared for you."

She opened the wardrobe, took out a package and slowly unfolded it. It was my new clothes for Chinese New Year - a child size, army uniform.

At that time, the army was admired by everyone so army uniform was very popular, in its green khaki or gray colors. It was difficult to get the chance to be a soldier, but army regalia influenced the styles of a generation who worshipped the uniform, and the colors that symbolized power, activism and rights.

I did love the dignity and glory of the red star on the army cap. It was hard to obtain a real army uniform, but because it meant so much, some people had them tailor-made.

But now I was not happy with it and this confused my mother.

"This is your favorite every year," she said.

"I like Sun's kind of clothes!"

"You are a boy!"

"I like bright colors."

"That is capitalism!"

"I do not mind, I like those clothes!"

"No!" By now my mother was shouting.

I began to cry.

"I'll give it to someone else!" she warned.

I cried louder but it changed nothing.

"Shame on you!"

My brother and sister laughed at me. They were both Red Guards, proudly dressing in army uniform.

After that, I went to Sun's home even more often than before, consoling myself in our costumed games. I loved to dress in different clothes - the fun and magic they provided more than compensated for their poor fit.

They surrounded me with shining colors. I felt like a butterfly, flying wild over the flowers in nature.

"Why does the prince look like a princess?"

Sun and her sisters giggled at me. I looked a bit ridiculous in feminine clothes, but we liked to play the game again and again.

Sometimes when I thought about it later at home and laughed aloud, Mother would warn me.

"You should not laugh like that!"

"Why not?"

"Someone will report you!"

Chapter 3

One day, Sun was crying when I arrived.

"What happened?" I asked.

She did not reply; just held her dog, Prince, in her arms. Her oldest sister Moon told me that someone had killed Sun's favorite cat, Princess.

"They hung Princess in the fig tree," said Moon.

The fig tree was years old and produced fruit during summer and autumn when Jing picked the figs and cooked them with sugar crystals to make syrup for her family. Sun shared it with me and it tasted wonderful.

I was the only child outside of the family who had a chance to taste that syrup. Other children were jealous of my privilege and complained. It was strange that Sun's was the only family to plant a fig tree in our town.

No one knew where the tree came from. It had suddenly appeared in the backyard of the house. Someone said that Sun's father brought it here from overseas, but no one could be sure.

At that moment, I was shocked by what Moon had told me. I did not know what to say. From the window on the second floor, I saw several branches of the fig tree now fractured and hanging lifelessly.

I tried to comfort Sun, "I'll ask my Grandpa to bring you another cat."

"But another cat is not Princess," Sun said to me.

What could I do to help her?

Jing came to her, "You cannot bring Princess back. But you still have Prince."

Sun stopped crying, holding Prince tightly in her arms.

Then Jing gave us the body. We took Princess to the riverside and selected a flat sandy field as her grave. It was a good place for Princess to rest in peace. I helped Sun to bury her.

Sun wrapped Princess in colorful sewing scraps and placed her in a cardboard box. We dug a hole in the sand, put the box inside and filled the hole with sand.

Sun spoke to Princess one last time.

'Now you can dream forever," she said.

"Maybe Princess will wake up and follow the stream to distant places..."

"She will drown."

"Cats have nine lives."

"What?"

"Grandma always says that..."

"If I find out who did this, I'll kill him!"

I tried to comfort Sun on the way home, but she was inconsolable.

At home, Jing said to Sun, "She's gone now and you have to move forward." She began telling fairy tales as she worked at her sewing. Gradually, the stories and the resilience of childhood helped Sun become happy again.

That evening, I told Mother about it while she cooked in the kitchen. I wanted to stay close to her. She joked that I was like a shadow following her everywhere. She was cooking and thinking at the same time.

"Baoguo, why don't you stay here at home?"

"I'm afraid alone."

"Your brother and sister are here. Why not play with them?"

I explained how my sister and brother always went outside to play-fight against others in Red Guards games. Mother listened as she chopped the vegetables. Father said nothing, just kept writing posters on the desk in the living room.

"It's better for you to stay at home."

"Why?"

"You ask too many questions. Why! Why!"

"Well...I..."

"Just stay at home! Don't ask me 'why' again!"

Mother had clearly lost her patience in her concern for me, so I shut my mouth and stood in silence. When the meal was ready, she put the dishes on the table and called the family to dinner.

Father was a serious man, so different from other men. He sat drinking alcohol in silence. He did not eat rice while drinking, only meat, egg, vegetables, and more alcohol. I thought that was a little strange.

There was no sound in the room, except our chewing. I was always afraid of him and dared not make eye-contact. Sometimes I could not resist speaking at the table, but he always shut me down.

"Do not talk during dinner!"

"Why not?"

I asked the question, even though I was afraid of him. His reply mystified me and he addressed his words, not to me, but to the air.

"A storm is coming."

"What do you mean?"

"Do not talk during dinner."

Mother tapped the dish with chopsticks, trying as always to restore balance - to ease the tensions between us at the table. I did not speak again but I was confused. What did a storm have to do with my question? It seemed unrelated.

At bedtime, I asked Mother about it, but she said nothing. That night I lay staring up at the mosquito net, unable to sleep. Father was snoring in another room with a sound like distant thunder.

Chapter 4

Princess's death was just the beginning. Sun told me that the fig tree itself was felled in the night. She had no idea who was responsible.

"Prince barked all night..."

"Fuck!"

I shouted from the window of the second floor. Never again could I stand here watching the green leaves and branches shaking in the wind and stretching towards me.

I remembered Sun reaching out her hand to pick the figs and giving one to me.

"Fresh.Taste it!" she'd said.

The sweetness drenched my mouth and throat, but also my heart.

Now, it was gone.

Sun's father Ahn had cleared away the mess leaving nothing but the stump. The backyard seemed empty now. Sun and her sisters stayed inside, helping their mother at her sewing.

The only sound was the sewing machine. Jing's face was serious as she worked. There were no fairy tales that day, no laughter or giggles. I stayed for a while, but the silence soon sent me home.

As I walked home wondering who might have destroyed the tree, I encountered my classmate Fatty who was so jealous of my friendship with Sun, yet now seemed happy to walk beside me.

"No more figs eh?" he teased.

"Who did it?"

"That would be telling . . ."

"Son of a bitch!"

"Only Revolutionary Masses would dare to do it."

I snarled at him. "They should be whipped!"

I left him and ran for home.

When I told Mother about it at dinner time, she seemed angry and a little worried.

"I warned you to stay home!" she said.

Father shot me a serious glance.

I bowed my head and ate faster. My sister and brother giggled at me until Father glowered at them warningly.

"We are Red Guards already," they said.

"But, you'll always be my children!"

The dogs barked all that night and the next. It went on for days.

"Prince barked all night too," said Sun, "but he never did before."

"I have seen them," said Fatty.

"Who?"

"A crew."

"They search at night."

"What for?"

"They hunt dogs!"

Rumors were spreading. Several people had died of rabies, so official teams were hunting dogs.

"Rabies!" said Fatty.

"Bullshit! Son-of-a-bitch, they just want to eat dog meat!"

I knew this because I remembered what had happened years before when Grandpa had promised to bring me a puppy. He loved me and tried to keep his promise. Then Mother told me that Grandpa had heard about an available puppy. He had gone to collect it for me, even though it was far from home.

I ran over the bridge towards my Grandparents' home to see if Grandpa had come back with my puppy. What color would he be? How big? How old? What would he look like?

When I arrived, Grandpa was already home but he was angry and there was no puppy.

"Those sons of bitches ate him!'

I almost collapsed. My puppy was in the bellies of the hunters.

The only thing I could be sure of was the puppy's gender.

"The dog had balls!" said Grandpa.

But Grandpa was elderly, almost blind. How could I trust his description of the puppy's appearance, its color, and size?

"It was a dirty thing to do!" he said of the dog hunter.

But he could only rage about it secretly. No one could resist the City Council's decisions.

Now I told Sun what had happened to my puppy, so she would look after Prince more carefully. Of course my story made her anxious. We discussed several plans. Then I helped her to block the dog's exit hole with bricks to keep Prince locked inside the house.

Prince was unhappy. That exit hole was his link to freedom. He jumped and barked around us as we worked.

"Quiet Prince!"

Sun's voice was low and her expression serious. But Prince just kept running and barking inside the house, trying to find a way out. He did not understand why we were doing this.

It made us both anxious. So Jing made a mask for Prince with scraps of sewing. He did not like it and tried to get rid of it, but failed. His voice was eerily muffled inside the mask.

Over the next few days, the barking of dogs faded suddenly from our town. There was an odd atmosphere. I could almost smell it, and at night, I could not sleep because I sensed a mystery presence secretly patrolling the streets.

I held my mother tightly.

"Is it the dog hunters?" I asked her.

A few days later, she told me that Grandpa's neighbor's dog had been taken by the dog hunter. Fatty had witnessed it and later he described it to me.

"The dog hunter tracked the dog through the streets. Then he roped it by the neck, and beat it to death with a hammer. He hung the body on a pole, burnt off its coat, washed it, cut it open and chopped it to pieces. They were eating and drinking, shouting and laughing all night."

I cursed them, "I hope they die of rabies!"

I repeated the story to Sun. She asked me if I could hide Prince in the home of my relatives in the countryside. I asked my Grandparents to help. But, Grandpa had no safe place in his village either.

"They search everywhere!" he said.

Sun could do nothing but hide Prince at home. Prince was forced to wear the mask all the time and stay leashed in the corner of the house. He wailed sadly as he watched us at play.

Before Prince had always taken part in our games, happily chasing and barking. But- now he could only sit and watch. Soon we stopped playing ourselves and just sat reading comic books.

It was boring and silent in the house, now that Jing no longer told fairy tales, but I still liked to visit, even just for the pleasure I found in the sound of the sewing machine.

In my eyes, Jing was a magician, feeding simple pieces of colorful cloth into the sewing machine to transform them into complex and beautiful clothes.

Her flying fingers were as white as a baby's, as they worked their delicate magic to the whirring of the machine. It was a mesmerizing sound.

"How long have you done this work?" I asked her.

Jing smiled. "Many years."

Sun said, "I'd like to be a tailor one day."

"I'm glad to hear it!" said Jing.

"You have a real gift," I told Jing.

Chapter 5

Although we tried so hard to protect Prince and keep him safe, we failed in the end. He was anonymously denounced and to our sorrow and anger, he was finally killed. We guessed that the dog-hunters had taken him secretly when the family was out of the house.

I suspected Fatty of being the informer and when I encountered him I cursed him.

"Fuck you asshole!"

Fatty was confused at first and denied my charge.

"I did nothing to Prince!"

But, I did not believe him. His father Lee was a chef for the City Council; I always joked that Fatty was fat because of his father's work. How had Fatty heard about the dog-hunters so much earlier than us? Could Lee be a dog hunter too?

We'd put out rumors that Prince had been sent to a countryside village. Everyone had forgotten him and no one suspected that he was hiding in the house all along.

I had leaked the secret to Fatty in a careless moment just a few days before it happened. No-one else knew where Prince was hiding, except Sun's family members, and me. Fatty was the only one who could have given away our secret.

"Wasn't me!" He continued to deny.

"Was so!" I insisted.

Our anger escalated into fighting. I drew first blood with scratches to his face and head, but I was no rival for his weight and strength and in the end I had to run to escape him. At least I had the speed advantage.

He shouted at me, "I'll kill you like a dog!"

But he did not chase me.

I ran home with a bloody nose. Mother screamed at the sight of me and took my face in her hands.

"What happened?"

She found a cloth and began cleaning my face.

"Fatty is an asshole!"

"Keep away from him. Keep out of trouble!"

I tried to explain what had happened, but she just kept repeating her order to keep out of all trouble. As I went to my bedroom to view my wounded nose in the mirror, she sent one last warning after me.

"If you get in trouble again, I'll beat you!"

Father was silent for a while, but his face was serious. Was he angry with me too? He ordered me coldly to take cigarettes to Grandpa.

"And get straight home afterwards," Mother warned.

I went out, swearing silently to myself. My parents were so unfair.

I could not help comparing my father with Sun's father Ahn. I knew Ahn always supported Sun. If she was in a situation like this, he would provide nothing but comfort.

"We all back you!" he would say.

But my Father only said, "Remember, we are nobody, we must be careful every moment."

Comparing Sun's parents to my own, depressed me. I pushed it from my thoughts.

I did not know Ahn very well. I just knew he was a teacher who taught English courses in high school. He used to shut himself inside his work-shop, reading English texts or pursuing his hobby.

His hobby was fishing, so he made fishhooks, some for himself, and some to sell. He was the only person in our town with this skill, so other fishermen needing hooks would buy them from him.

Sometimes when I was there playing with his daughters, Ahn would be quietly reading; sometimes, I heard hammering inside his workshop.

Jing explained that Ahn had learned his hobby overseas, years ago. Sometimes he gave me a fishhook as a gift. I liked the sharp efficiency of those hooks and their beautiful shape.

And now as I passed along the riverbank on my father's errand to Grandpa with the cigarettes, I saw Ahn himself sitting under the willow tree, smoking and watching the surface of the water.

I hesitated, then walked towards him and stood close. Without looking up from the water, he signaled me to sit beside him.

I was nervous because he was a teacher. He continued to focus on the gleaming water. I needed to break the silence between us.

"About Prince...?"

He sighed and turned his eyes my way, then stared in shock when he saw the state of my face.

"What happened to you?"

"It's nothing."

I had caught his attention at least. I explained what had caused my injuries.

"Children should not fight," he said.

It made him sound like a teacher again. Mother and Father had told me that adults fought wars. And I had even seen neighbors squabbling.

"But adults fight," I said. "Do you ever need to, in your work at school?"

He shook his head, "I don't like violence. It is no good for anyone."

"But you returned to China for the Revolution?"

"Yes, but I am just a teacher, teaching English."

"Oh."

Then he changed the subject to fishing, describing it as a sport requiring great patience. I did not understand.

"Fishing is a sport?"

"Yes."

As far as I knew fishing was no more than a way to get meat. We did it for no other reason.

"Overseas it's a kind of sport." Said Ahn. "They do it not just for meat, but for fun and health!" He went on to describe how people in distant countries fished to relax in a natural environment, or to seek adventure, or even to compete - to match their skills against other fishermen. Often, they had no need of the meat.

Incredible! It seemed so strange to me.

Suddenly, the buoy bobbed in the water. Ahn stopped talking and worked his fishing rod. The reel sang as he wound in his catch. And it was a big one. Ahn smiled as he dragged the fish close to shore and netted it.

Ahn was respected in our town for the fishing gear he made from wood and bamboo. No one could do it like he could. My brother and I had both tried and both failed.

I reached out to touch the fish and Ahn saw the cigarette box in my hand.

"Hey! Children should not smoke."

"My father sent me to take these to my Grandpa."

"Your Grandpa?"

"Yes."

He became thoughtful for a few seconds. Then he handed the fish to me. I hesitated to take it.

"What...?"

"This fish is for your Grandpa too. I have more than one."

"But..."

"Remember? I go fishing, but not just for the meat."

I took the fish and hit the road again. By now the wind had strengthened and I had ignored Mother's advice to wear more clothes. I began to run towards my destination.

Grandpa welcomed me warmly and Grandma put something into my hand, then started cooking in the kitchen. What had she given me?

"White Rabbit!"

White Rabbit was my favorite brand of candy. The taste was wonderful - so sweet and milky and the wrapper had a funny picture of a rabbit with buck teeth.

At that time, everything in our daily life was rationed by the authorities. People needed stamps to buy goods. My Grandparents always said that candy was bad for their teeth, but, actually, they had no teeth. I knew she had saved them specially for me.

When she'd finished cooking, Grandma served lunch. Grandpa joked with me. "How can a blind old man manage this fish?"

I'd forgotten his eyesight was bad.

"Don't worry. I can help," I said.

I rolled up my sleeves and served out the fish.

"Oh, we have to eat. Your mouth is watering!"

Grandpa ate his fish very slowly and carefully. We pulled out the small fish-bones with our teeth and fingers. Grandma laughed at me. Both of them were happy.

Suddenly I asked, "Can you bring me a puppy?"

My Grandpa cursed the dog hunter.

"That son of a bitch killed all the dogs!"

After lunch, I stayed and chatted with them for a while. Grandpa told me a secret that before public-private partnerships, they'd had their own tofu business for many years.

Grandma described their old career to me, getting up earlier than anyone else, milling the soya beans, cooking them and squeezing the milk. Grandpa said it was a hard work.

"But it was our own business."

"You were the boss?"

"We were. But we had to hand it over to the authorities..."

"Why?"

"It was the right thing to do. If we kept it, we would become of the Five Types of People straight away."

"But why?"

"You ask too many questions, silly boy."

But now their business was no more than a memory. It made no sense to me, but I did not stop worry about it. I glanced at the wall clock and said goodbye to them.

As I walked home I thought of the puppy I longed for but never could have. Candy was the best consolation my Grandparents could offer me, but it hardly compared with a puppy. There was a big difference between the reality and the ideal.

Chapter 6

With no dogs barking the silence seemed unreal.

A rumour was spreading that a child had been abducted by a stranger. Thieves were active in the town. It made everyone feel unsafe. Mother told me to stay home to act as a 'watchdog'.

I argued, but Mother said it was an order and must be obeyed. At home I was bored in no time and soon slipped out to play with Sun.

She was still sad about losing Prince. I sympathized. Prince was not just our playmate, but had always been an effective watchdog.

"They robbed my house last night."

Jing had discovered the theft that morning. The thieves had worked so quietly, no one heard a sound

"They were good at their job! They did not break windows."

"How could they do that?"

"They used a long stick with a hook."

"Oh...like... fishing..."

"...the window was open..."

"What was stolen?"

"Some clothes hanging close to the window, including my skirt, and... underwear."

Suddenly, she stopped talking about it, and blushed. Then I too blushed.

At that moment, we missed Prince very much. He not only guarded his own home, but also the neighbors'. Because of Prince, stealing had never been a problem near us. But now he was gone. What made it worse was that we never saw his body.

We guessed someone had eaten Prince, probably the dog hunters. Sometimes, when one of them passed me, I spat at them behind their backs.

"Remember the story Jing told us?" I said to Sun. "When the wolf ate the little girl but she jumped out alive? I wish Prince could do that."

"The real world is not like a fairy tale," she said.

How I longed for those lost days when we listened to fairy tales and Prince was alive, barking and howling, and there was so much to laugh about.

But things got worse.

One morning, the local authorities broadcast the news by loud-speaker, that a thief was being held captive in the backyard of the town hall. We were curious.

I went with Sun to have a look. People crowded around the thief who was chained to a tree. It was noisy there. I squeezed through the crowds and stood near him.

The thief was handsome, about twenty years old, naked and strong, his skin shining in the sunlight. Items of clothing hung from his neck; he must have stolen them. His legs and feet were bare except for the leg-irons holding him in place.

The thief was singing a song of grief. Obviously it was not the Revolutionary Songs we listened to every day. This was an original tune - like a wind blowing over me, fresh from the distance.

Voices in the crowd spoke out against him.

"He is young and strong. He can work for his needs."

"He should not steal. He deserves no sympathy."

The anger intensified into physical assault. People slapped his face with palm fronds as a lesson to their sons; children kicked his legs; young men punched his belly with their fists.

Then, bricks began to fly.

His blood flowed.

But the thief sang on, ignoring his persecutors, his voice ringing out over all their screams of rage. His lament seemed to spread from the backyard of the town hall until it echoed throughout the town.

Sun burst into tears and ran away. I followed close behind her. But the song of the thief followed the both of us. No matter how far and fast we ran we could still hear his song resounding in our ears. We closed the door at last to shut out that terrible scene, then gasped and coughed to get our breath back.

"He is crazy!"

"How could that happen?"

"Shame on him!"

We told Jing what we had seen. She stopped her work at once and gave us her full attention as we described what had happened to the thief.

"It is never worth it to steal," she said. "But if he stole only clothes - it's not that bad. They're only objects."

She stopped and looked thoughtful. Then she said, "Perhaps that poor man has a mental illness. I'd be happy to send him some clothes. He should just ask."

I thought of the beautiful clothes that Jing sewed.

"If I ask will you give me some too?"

"What did you say?" said Jing.

I mumbled vaguely, aware of my slip-up, to ask such a thing at a time like that.

"What?" said Jing again.

I said nothing, just shook my head. My face was hot.

That evening, I told Mother the whole story, while she cooked in the kitchen. She pressed her palm to her chest and kept saying "My God.." and she made many mistakes in her cooking that night.

During dinner, Father complained that Mother had put too much salt in this or not enough in that, and he seemed anxious, but did not say why. He just kept drinking and eating.

"The thief is hateful, he deserved a good beating!" said my brother.

He and my sister seemed intrigued by the story. Had they been there watching too? I could have missed them in all the chaos or perhaps they arrived after we ran off. I would not be surprised. It was the kind of thing they wouldn't want to miss.

My father growled, "Quiet all of you! This was not your business. Don't watch things like this. Never get involved with any mob, ever!"

When my brother tried to speak, Father silenced him again. Then, he turned to glare at me, his eyes blood shot from drinking. I was afraid of him. I bowed my head to avoid eye-contact.

"Did you hear what I just said?"

"...well..."

"Yes or no?"

Mother stared at me. I nodded to show I understood. But that was not good enough for her.

"Answer your father!" she said.

I spoke out word by word. "Yes - I - heard - you. I - understand."

Then, Mother turned to my sister and brother and insisted they both answer in the same way.

They obeyed. She sighed deeply.

Chapter 7

On Saturday morning, I invited Sun to come with me to see if anything was happening in the school grounds. But Sun had to spend time with relatives who were visiting her family. I walked alone towards the school.

I went along the river, passing by the town hall. There was a bulletin board at the hall and I wanted to see the latest messages published there. I approached the board to read the papers on display.

There were announcements about some "traitors" or "counter-revolutionaries" or "spies" who had been sentenced to execution by firing squad. As my eyes scanned the names on the list the only sound I could hear was the soft flapping of the torn papers in the wind.

Suddenly, a poster about a stage drama caught my eye. This was what I had hoped to find. I read it quickly. It was one of the famous revolutionary model dramas called The Red Detachment of Women. It was coming soon to our town.

The show was good news for us. I was so excited about it, I suddenly needed to take a piss before continuing my journey, happier for the news. At least until I thought about what else I'd seen on that board.

The names in black ink with the ominous red crosses over them. All of those people were doomed.

Red crosses meant death.

Black crosses meant, "Watch out! This person is bad."

Suddenly, my thoughts slipped to the bloodied thief and I felt sick, so I walked faster to escape the memory, hurrying on towards the school.

The campus was always crowded and noisy on weekdays with students everywhere, chasing and yelling. In summer, cicadas and birds sang in the treetops over our heads.

Those trees so full of birds and insects formed huge green shade umbrellas that rustled with life in the wind. Their shade created cool havens from the summer heat.

Now, everything was quiet and empty with doors and windows locked; posters flapped from walls or hung from strings between the trees. In the eerie stillness, the wind crackling through paper was the only sound to be heard.

Then I heard something in the distance. I looked around and saw a crowd of people; still far off but coming this way, many carrying red flags and placards. They came closer and soon they were pouring into the school grounds, destroying the silence.

"What's going on?" I asked.

"They're holding an assembly here."

Someone set up a rostrum on the stage in the center of the campus. They covered a long table with a red cloth, positioned a microphone and loud-speakers, placed the cordons. They tested the microphone by tapping it with a finger.

The militias forced some men and women to walk into the classroom.

Revolutionary Songs burst into life through the loud-speakers. It made me jump. Should I stay or should I go home? Curiosity won out. I stayed.

The crowd and its noise was growing by the moment, becoming a spectacle with the energy of a school sports event, and yet it made me nervous for reasons I could not explain. Was it just the excitement?

I moved through the crowd towards my classroom and looked through the window. The chairs and tables had been piled up in a corner of the room.

People in black clothes, squatted on the ground in another corner, heads bowed, faces somber. I knew they must be the bad ones. Perhaps they were landlords, rich peasants, anti-Revolutionaries, gang busters or rightists. They were labeled by the unifying term "Five Types of People." Our teacher had taught us about it.

Armed militias guarded them; two more guarded the entrance, guns in their hands.

They shouted at me.

"Go away!"

I walked away in fright. Suddenly, the voice of the assembly host was shouting through the loud-speakers.

"Attention!"

"Silence, please!"

"Attention!"

"I declare the Critical Assembly open!"

The voice was harsh but people responded. They sat on the floor and gave their attention to the host. He coughed for a few seconds, his face aglow, then began to read from his paper manuscript, raising up his fists while shouting.

His passion spread like fire, through the anxious crowds in the school campus. They imitated him, raising up their fists, shouting aloud until the noise rolled like thunder across the sky resounding throughout the school and beyond. It shocked and deafened me.

The oratory of the host brought the crowd to its feet, whipping everyone to chaos. I could see nothing, above the shoulders and heads, because I was shorter than others, so I squeezed my way closer to the stage.

The "Five Types of People" were taken to the rostrum, forced to kneel at the edge of the stage, facing the crowds. The militias had tied their hands behind them - like birds with trapped wings. It reminded me of the way Father trussed his chickens just before he killed them.

The assembly host raised his fist to shout at the captives; the crowd followed his example. The "Five Types of People" all bowed their heads down, hiding their faces behind long dirty hair, silent in shame.

The assembly host shouted his accusations louder than ever and the crowd echoed his cries. The militias grabbed the captives by their hair pulling back their heads to show their faces to everyone. The crowd roared for blood.

At that moment, I saw several people stood on the stage, having down-cast but immobile faces. Then, zealots rushed up with bricks to attack the "Five Types of People," whose blood was soon flowing on the stage.

I thought I might pass out. I had to run away, to escape that crowd. I ran back to the town center hoping to rest there. But, the sound of a truck engine and the noise of the crowd seemed to follow me.

I waited, confused. The truck was coming my way. Then I remembered that this was the time for public exhibition of the captives. It was routine after all such meetings.

The "Five Types of People" were still bound as before and guarded by militias with guns but now there were cards hanging on their chests announcing their name and their crime. The names had big red or black crosses.

The Jie Fang brand truck continued along the main street of the town center. More crowds were gathering on both sides of the street, condemning and throwing stones at the "Five Types of People".

I heard one of the militias shout at someone.

"What the fuck! You hit me, you idiot!"

People laughed aloud.

Some of the "Five Types of People" tried to avoid the missiles thrown at them; others hardly seemed to care, as though they knew that death was the next step in their journey and would come either today or another day soon.

I squeezed out from the crowds and ran for home.

Chapter 8

I ran until I was out of breath.

I encountered Sun at the corner of the street near her home. She noticed my panic.

"What happened to you?"

I could only gasp and mumble in reply.

"What are you saying?"

I tried to calm my breathing. It took time to recover enough to try to explain to Sun what had happened.

"Things...in the school campus..."

"Your teeth are chattering!"

"...I...well..."

"You're shaking!"

"...fuck..."

It wasn't easy to speak when my feet could hardly support my body. I squatted, vomiting and coughing. I took deep breaths, hoping it would help me stand up again.

But I could not stop my teeth from chattering. Sun knelt before me; her anxiety plain.

I closed my eyes but it seemed a long time before my shaking calmed enough for me to describe what I had witnessed to her. Even then I had to drag out each word one at time.

When I finished at last, I wanted to vomit again, but could only cough and retch. Sun's face was pale. She said nothing, just squatted beside me. At last she stood, with some difficulty.

"Let's go!" she said weakly.

I stood up and followed her slowly. We were silent on the road, just wanting to get home as soon as possible.

In the doorway of Sun's house, we almost collided with Fatty's father Lee as he rushed out of the house with his head turned back to shout to Jing.

"You'll pay for this one day!"

Lee was angry, ignoring everything in front of him. He cursed Jing aloud, as he hurried off. Sun and I stood watching in shock until he disappeared at the corner of the street.

"Mother, what happened?"

Jing heard Sun's question but would make no reply. In the end we asked Sun's sisters what had led to such a scene.

They explained that Lee had commissioned his overalls, a few days ago. Jing made them as carefully as she always did for him and for all her customers. But this time Lee would not be satisfied. He kept asking for one modification after another to the garment. Jing followed his orders every time.

But, there was no happy ending. Lee was well-known to drive a hard bargain. Even in his work as a chef he liked to take advantage of others. He refused to be satisfied with Jing's work and then disputed her fee.

When Jing insisted on fair payment he became angry and threatened her.

Jing suddenly sighed to us. "There are more and more people like that now."

Previously, when customers came to Jing to commission clothes, they were always polite, trusting Jing's reputation and sewing skill. Jing did her best work for them in return. Negotiations always ended happily on both sides of the deal.

Sometimes, when customers commented on the beautiful clothes she made for her family, she would offer to make something similar for them.

But always they would pass it off as a joke. Perhaps, though they liked Jing, they dared not accept the colorful clothes she offered them. Nobody took the joke seriously.

"Jing's family are different," they would say, "They came from overseas."

Yes, even Mother secretly admired Jing's colorful clothes, but dared not dress that way herself. She commissioned dark or gray-colored clothes for all of us. It made me unhappy, but, what could I do?

"Such clothes are too conspicuous in our town."

All I could do was dream about it. Like many others perhaps, I was secretly jealous of Jing's family and at that moment I felt a little guilty about that.

My train of thought was interrupted by Sun's voice. "Father, are you ok?"

I turned and saw Ahn arriving. He did not reply to Sun, just walked straight into his workshop and closed the door.

An awkward atmosphere spread through the house in the sudden silence that followed his arrival. I said goodbye to Sun, and left in hurry, but as I walked home, I wondered what had happened to Ahn.

Strangely, all my family members were already home when I arrived. Father and Mother seemed too tired to speak. But, my brother and sister were sitting in the bamboo sofa, chatting in low excited voices. They were discussing the assembly.

Father drank silently during dinner, eating vegetables and fried eggs. He seemed lost inside himself. We heard nothing from him but the sound of his chewing. Then Mother asked me where I had been today.

I froze. Then mumbled some reply that made no sense. Father was suddenly alert.

'Where have you been today?" he snapped.

I raised my head, turning to Mother.

"I...I have...been..."

"Answer me!"

"I ...have been...at the assembly."

Father put down his cup, stood up, walked to the corner by the door, picked up a bamboo stick and walked back to me.

I had no time to run away. He beat me hard. I cried aloud, hoping for Mother's sympathy. At that moment, only she could protect me.

Father shouted at me. "I warned you before!"

My brother was shocked at first, but then I saw him smile. My sister dared not speak. I ran and tried to hide behind Mother. She tried hard to stop Father.

Father yelled, "No next time, ok?"

But Father was not finished yet. Next he turned to my brother and gave him a good beating too. This was a respite for me and a surprise to my brother. Now at least I was not the only one to suffer.

Father thundered at him. "Did you forget your duty? I told you to look after your younger brother!"

At first, my brother bore his unexpected beating in silence but in the end he too burst into tears and ran to Mother to avoid the bamboo stick.

Father took full advantage of my brother and I being both in the same place. He beat me again, then gave my brother another turn, until our yells echoed through the house.

Mother could not protect both of us at the same time and while trying she occasionally got in the way of the bamboo stick herself. She did not blame Father for this and later she told us that he did it only for our benefit.

I thought that was ridiculous.

Chapter 9

The next morning, I rose earlier than usual because I was going with Grandma to collect firewood. We walked towards the mountains surrounding the town. It was a long hard walk for me just to reach them.

Mother worked hard in her daily life, and encouraged all of us to do the same, especially in physical labor. She thought it was good life experience for me to assist Grandma occasionally.

"You should prepare for your future."

I did not understand what she meant, but I was happy to follow her or Grandma and help them to collect firewood, or harvest sweet potato. It was hard physical labor, but I enjoyed it.

Besides, Sun told me that Jing had become so worried about the future that she no longer told fairy tales.

"What does she think will happen?"

"I don't know."

So I was happy to work with Grandma and leave Sun's family to themselves.

But it wasn't just Sun's family who wondered about the future. Everyone else waited in suspense and readiness for the guidance and orders that could come from Beijing at any moment.

"No one knows, except Chairman Mao."

Those words were on everyone's lips and it was not a joke. Everyone took it seriously. We trusted Chairman Mao more than our parents.

But at Sun's home the silence grew until the only sound still to be heard was the whirring of the sewing machine.

No wonder I preferred to spend the day with Grandma in the space and freedom of the mountains where I could breathe new air.

But before I'd walked far into the mountains, I was tired and hot. I stopped at the roadside to rest, wiping sweat from my face, waiting for the wind to cool me. Grandma hardly seemed to feel the miles we had covered. I admired her very much.

"Grandma, you are so strong!"

"You will be stronger too, when you are grown."

She smiled and comforted me. She always encouraged me to eat well so I would grow quickly. I too wanted to grow up and choose my own path in life, independent of Grandma or other adults.

I looked down from the mountain towards our town so far away sitting in its wide basin surrounded by mountains. From here the houses looked like matchboxes with the river flowing through like a shining ribbon.

As my eyes followed its course, I dreamed of one day escaping along the river to the outside world.

It had been done before, by fishermen boating to the big city so far away. Others had gone by car, along the dirt road. But I was only a child and such journeys were only dreams.

Grandma interrupted my thoughts. "Are you hungry?"

"A little."

"We'll rest now."

She sat on the ground and passed me the same lunch she always provided on our firewood expeditions - a sweet potato. I thought it was not soft enough but I kept my thoughts to myself.

The wind was blowing; at first it was a relief to feel it drying my sweat, but soon I began to feel chilled. After a while, Grandma glanced at the sky and stood up, managing her knife and shoulder pole.

"We should go now."

We continued our journey, crossing one mountain and then another to our destination. Then we performed the task we had so done many times before.

Grandma had a lifetime's experience of collecting fire wood. She cut the small trees down with her knife, gathering the pieces together.

I followed behind her, going back and forth, helping to carry the wood through the forest. It could be lonely at times and a little frightening, but there was always something interesting to discover.

I found many wild fruits which I tasted and appreciated, and also colourful mushrooms, appearing before me on the forest floor, then a wild rabbit fleeing by me in a panic to escape.

I wanted to chase the wild rabbit, but, I was afraid of losing myself in the forest, so I just stood there, listening to birdsong.

Finally, Grandma cut a maple tree for me to carry. I placed the trunk across my shoulders. Grandma tied our firewood into two bundles and hung them from each end of her bamboo shoulder pole. We set off for home.

Exhaustion and the heavy load made the journey home seem longer. After a long walk, we rested beside a creek. The stream was clear and the water so inviting, I washed the sweat from my forehead and face and squatted down to drink.

I noticed a sweet smell. "Flowers," I said to Grandma. She smiled, walked to an osmanthus tree beside the creek and picked some flowers for me. I put them close to my face and for one instant I breathed that wonderful perfume before it blew away in the wind. I placed them into the pocket on my chest, so the scent would accompany me along the journey home.

Grandma was sweating. Her heavy dark-colored clothes were sticking to her skin. Surely she would have been more comfortable wearing light-coloured clothes made from lighter fabrics.

"Grandma, do you have any colourful clothes?"

"They are unsuitable for physical labor."

I was not sure about that. Colourful clothes made me feel happy and comfortable. Grandma smiled at me.

"You are just a child."

After a short rest, Grandma stood.

"We must go now," she said. "Staying any longer will only make it harder to get started again. Let's go!"

I wanted to stay right there on the ground, but I had to follow her again. Just as our town came into view in the distance, my belly began to churn. I had to slow down, and then squat on the ground, holding my belly.

"What's wrong with you?" she asked

"...Pain..."

"Might be the creek water?"

Grandma stopped, unloaded her burden and crouched in front of me, checking my body. But, she was not a doctor and could not solve the problem.

"Hold on, we'll be home soon."

I felt a bit better after a short rest. Grandma encouraged me onwards. I squatted again, but continued the journey. All we could do was keep going forward.

Occasionally Grandma asked me how I felt. I had no strength to reply - it might cost me too much energy. I was afraid to glance at our town still so far away. Was I going to die? I just kept my head down and moved forward one step at a time as best I could.

Grandma tried to reassure me. "After you have slept, you will be fine."

The hard journey ended when we finally arrived at Grandma's home. Grandma made a cup of sugar water for me, and when I'd finished it, she insisted I lie down in the bed. Why did Mother and Grandma always dose me on sugar water whenever I was unwell?

Mother came to collect me the same evening. Mother and Grandma both praised me for my courage to survive so hard a journey.

"Well done!"

"He's the best!"

The suffering had been a new experience for me and I never forgot that day because I was proud I'd found the strength to endure. But somehow, I could not stop thinking about death.

"Mother, what if I died?"

"That's not going to happen."

She hugged me tenderly to reassure me.

That night, after a refreshing shower, my sleep was too deep for any dreams or nightmares.

Chapter 10

My brother told me quietly Ahn had been suspended from his duties at school because of his overseas background. It seemed ridiculous. Ahn was considered an excellent teacher.

"You told me that Ahn is the best."

"He was."

"What can he do now? "

He mimicked an adult tone."Now? He must find other employment!"

"But..."

"Oh, you are such a child!"

He gave a superior smile, said no more and went out, leaving me alone at home, still thinking about Ahn's situation.

I could make no sense of it, so I went to Sun for confirmation. I met her suddenly when I was half way there. In fact we almost collided at the corner of the street. She was in a hurry and seemed unhappy, walking with head bowed and carrying a lunch box in her hand.

"Where are you going?"

She did not answer me, continuing on her way. She would not stop beside me so I followed her to the riverside. Ahn was there, sitting in the shadow of the willow tree, fishing in peace.

I could imagine my brother teasing, "He seems happy enough."

We did not disturb him at first - just stood and watched from close by. When he finally noticed us there, he turned and smiled. Sun gave him the lunchbox and sat beside him; I remained standing.

"Hey! Sit down please!"

"Why?"

"Fish won't bite if they see you there."

Ahn's joke made me relax, and I sat quietly beside Sun.

Ahn sat without a word, watching the surface of the water.

Sometimes, floating objects caught on the fishing line and he would move the rod a little to dislodge them. But mostly Ahn just waited, motionless. It seemed he was waiting, not only for the fish but also for something else beyond our understanding. His eyes stared at the water as though he might lose himself in it.

The wind blew through the willow leaves sweeping them over the surface of the water. Some willow leaves dropped into the river and its flow carried them far away downstream.

"Father, you should have lunch now."

"Ok. In a minute."

But still he ignored the lunchbox. After a while, Sun opened it for him. Ahn accepted it from her, but he ate only a little before continuing with thoughts that carried his soul far from the food and the fishing and anything else that lay before his eyes.

It was not the first time I had seen Ahn sunk in a daydream. But still no one could deny that he was the best teacher in the school. Not only that, he was the only English teacher in our town. Students liked his English course very much.

His colleagues liked to tease him.

"The only time your day-dreams stop is when you teach."

But no one thought it was a problem. Ahn was a nice guy who would never harm a soul. Despite his daydreams, he was responsible, hard-working and always punctual.

My brother was one of Ahn's students. He often told me about Ahn's classes. But, strangely he had no wish to visit his teacher's home.

"I get enough teaching at school. I don't need any extra."

Was that the real reason? I had my doubts. For me, Sun's home was a wonderful place, full of fun and happiness.

"You're only a child!" my brother would say.

He and I saw things from very different angles.

My train of thought returned to the riverbank as the conversation between Ahn and Sun revived suddenly. Her words were hesitant.

"Father - you should go home now."

"I want to stay here for a while, alone."

Sun swallowed her words. She was silent for a while, then stood and walked away, sighing. I followed behind her quietly, one step after another, plucking up the courage to ask my question.

"Is it true?"

She did not answer me just then.

But days later, Sun told me it was true.

"He is not fired?"

"They told him it is only temporary."

She tried to explain. That day, when the teachers were in a meeting, the assembly host reported the latest directive from Chairman Mao which had arrived the previous night. One teacher must be chosen as the 'rightist' of the school.

The host stressed his point. "We must choose someone now!"

No one dared to leave the meeting for fear of being chosen while they were out of the room. All avoided one another's eyes.

The hours passed and the tension in the atmosphere increased.

Suddenly, Ahn could wait no longer. He moved from his chair, rushing out to the toilet. He needed to relieve not only his bladder, but also his bowel. He was suffering from a sudden attack of diarrhea. He was a gentleman. Not for any reason would he lose control of bodily functions in public.

By the time he returned to the meeting he had been chosen as the rightist. The assembly host announced the result, and everyone could relax at last and leave the meeting. They all rushed to the toilet. Ahn was not the only one who had held on too long.

"That's how it happened." said Sun.

I swore.

Sun closed her story by saying, "Father said he would rather die, than lose control in public."

That evening, I could not resist repeating it all to my family. They felt sorry for Ahn and sighed for him. We discussed his story quietly, with many thoughtful pauses separating our comments.

"He should not have left the meeting."

"It's hard to hold on for so long."

"What can we learn from this?"

"I know...You should not drink too much."

"I understand..."

"But you...will you stop?"

Mother stared at Father with an anxious face. He hesitated for a moment, and then raised the cup and drained it, savoring every drop, as though he knew it might be his last chance. He picked up his chopsticks, took fried eggs from the dish, chewed them noisily and swallowed.

"I only drink at home..."

"There's something else to learn from this," said Mother. "Never drink water before any meeting!"

"What?"

But Mother had the last word.

"Remember!"

Chapter 11

Soon afterwards, Ahn was sent to do a course at the Cadre School for Learning. He was told that he must have a shower to rinse off his impure thoughts. What could that mean?

"A shower?"

"To wash dirty thoughts away."

After that, Sun's house seemed different. Although Ahn had never played with us directly, we had always been aware of his presence among us, as he worked at his hobby in his workshop nearby. Now he was gone, we missed him.

"Is the school far away?"

"It may be couple of hours' journey."

"Driving or just walking?"

"He walked, carrying a package."

"What was in it?"

"Just things he might need, if he gets a chance to teach again there."

Sun said that her family could do nothing except pray for him. Orders were orders, and no one could disobey. People at that time were increasingly restricted by one order or another controlling their daily lives.

More and more people came to commission new clothes for Chinese New Year, keeping Jing hard at work every day. Sun's sisters Moon and Star helped Jing at her tasks.

Normally, Sun and I chatted quietly or read comic books in the next room. I could hear the whirring of the machine from the sewing room. Once, those sounds had mixed with Ahn's reading or hammering; but not anymore.

Sometimes, I looked over Sun's shoulders to the cutting table. It looked a little messy. Moon worked there now, cutting out the pieces for the clothes. When Jing stopped sewing to iron the finished clothes, Moon took her place at the sewing machine.

Much had changed.

The sewing room was full of dreary fabrics producing dull and colorless clothes The colourful clothes had retreated to the edges, hanging forgotten in the shadows.

I walked to the window of the second floor and looked out at the cloudy sky. Wild geese flew by, their wings forming V shapes like the Chinese character "人". I watched until they disappeared into the clouds.

"Winter is coming," I said.

"Yes, I feel a chill in the air," said Sun from behind me in the room.

I looked down at the empty space where the fig tree had been, remembering the delicious taste of the fig syrup that Jing used to make in summer and autumn in the past. Sometimes, Mother made syrup for us too, but it had only sweetness, without any of the wonderful fruit flavor.

"Where did your fig tree come from Sun?"

"Somewhere far from here," she sighed.

There was a long silence in the room.

"I have to go home now," I said at last.

Suddenly I spotted movement in the distance. Father- and there was someone with him. I rushed away, hoping to reach home before Father.

"Say hello to Uncle Chen."

"Ah, you've grown!" said Uncle Chen.

"How are you?" I said.

Uncle Chen was happy to meet me, stroking my head, comparing me to last time he'd seen me. It made me feel shy. Uncle Chen was very friendly with Father, but he lived far away from us in a village surrounded by mountains.

I remembered previous times when Uncle Chen visited with gifts produced in the mountains where he lived. He would arrive, have lunch and chat with Father. Then he would head home carrying goods his own village was short of.

"Where have you come from?" I asked him.

"Red Star village."

"Is that very far?"

"Oh, yes."

"How many kilometers?"

My question confused Uncle Chen. He hesitated, thinking.

"It takes me half a day to get here."

It explained why he always started home straight after lunch.

"Is there any school over there?"

I'm not sure why I asked him that. I just did. Perhaps it was because Sun had told me that the Cadre School was also far from our town. I wondered if Uncle Chen knew it.

"School?"

"Yes."

"There is no school for children like you, but there is one for grown-ups."

"For grown-ups?"

"Let me think about it... oh, yes... it's called Cadre School."

So he did know it! I didn't speak, hoping he would say more.

"It is a Training Camp, just near the village. Why did you ask?"

"My neighbor has gone there for a learning course."

My father chose that moment to interrupt and he spoke with a warning tone.

"Off you go now," he said, "It's my turn to chat to Uncle Chen!"

I shut up at once, and being a little hungry, I went to the kitchen. I found sweet potatoes in a saucepan and ate one, washing it down with a scoop of water from the big water jar.

I saw a package on the ground in the corner of the kitchen. I went to it and opened it to find bamboo shoots. This must be the gift that Uncle Chen had brought. Mother always fried bacon with it, creating a flavor I loved. The cooking smell always reminded me of festivals, especially the Chinese New Year.

Next day, I reported to Sun what Uncle Chen had told me about the Cadre Training Camp.

"Perhaps Ahn will write to us from there soon," she said.

"Of course, he should write to you, soon."

"He's been gone so long. We've heard nothing yet."

Her face was clouded by anxiety for her father. These days, she was less physically active but more emotional than before. I asked her what was on her mind, but, she just said it was nothing.

It was strange how the shadows hanging over her seemed only to make her more beautiful than ever.

Chapter 12

A few days later, one Saturday afternoon, I suddenly encountered Ahn himself in the street. I was in town to buy soy sauce for Mother and to my surprise, there he was coming towards me.

He looked like a farm or factory worker, wearing dark clothes, a black cloth cap, two bamboo shoots hanging from his neck in front, and a yellow canvas bag on his back. I could hardly recognize him. He spoke to me.

"Hey, where are you going?"

"I..."

I was too shocked by his unexpected appearance to answer his question properly. He did not stop, just smiled and passed me by, walking quickly towards his house.

I stood watching until he disappeared around the corner of the street. Ahn was going home!

"It will be a big surprise for them."

The family had received no letters from Ahn the whole time he'd been away. Sun would be thrilled to see him walking in the door.

I quickly finished my errand and returned home to tell Mother what I had seen. She listened but said nothing, too busy at her cooking. I stood nearby and watched her work.

Mother was an excellent cook. I liked to spend time before dinner watching her at work in the kitchen. The good smells were a promise of the wonderful food we would all soon be eating.

She had soaked the dried bamboo shoots overnight and now she chopped them into pieces. She chopped pork also. I knew that in just a few minutes, Uncle Chen's gift of dried bamboo shoots, would be transformed into a delicious meal.

My mouth was watering.

Mother scooped a small clot of white lard from a bowl into the pot, melted it, added pieces of ginger, heated them, added the pork first, then the chopped bamboo shoots. She flipped and mixed it all together, added a little water and put the lid on the pot.

The closed pot muffled the cooking sounds but when Mother removed the lid, steam rose and a wonderful smell filled the kitchen. My mouth watered more and more.

Next, she fried eggs and then some vegetables in the same oil.

"That is always the order."

"Why?"

"It saves oil!"

Mother worked on, letting me enjoy the experience alongside her. It was wonderful to just stand there breathing in all those delicious smells.

When the cooking was done, Mother called to tell the family it was ready. Then we noticed that Father was not home yet. We would have to wait before eating.

Mother could not sit still. She was anxious like before, coming in and out of the kitchen, washing a dish that was already clean, going out to see if he was coming, taking out the rubbish bag, anything to keep herself busy.

By this time, my mouth had been watering for far too long. I was so hungry my stomach was rumbling. I sat in the chair, staring longingly at the dishes on the table while the minutes ticked slowly by.

He arrived at last, thank God. Mother took his black bag from him and asked my brother and sister to help.

"What happened?"

Father explained his lateness. "We had a meeting after work."

He went to the kitchen. Mother followed him, filled a washbasin with water. I heard Father washing his face.

She chided him, "You frightened me!"

Father explained over dinner. Just at the end of the working day, the manager had received the latest high guidelines from Chairman Mao. The information must be conveyed to everyone at once, so there was an urgent meeting after work.

I had been eating hungrily but now as I listened my chewing slowed and stopped altogether. I took a breath, raised my head to look at the portrait of Chairman Mao on the wall. He smiled down on all of us with his mysterious smile, but how real was that smile and what did it hide?

Father drank too much wine too quickly and became a little drunk. Mother tried to persuade him to stop and go to bed early. Father ignored her at first, but went to the bedroom at last.

"Your father has been very tired lately," Mother explained.

With Father gone, the atmosphere at the table changed. I wanted to go outside. Sometimes if Father was not there, I could get away with taking my bowl outside, where I could eat and play at the same time. Mother reproached me for it, but did not stop me.

I carried my dinner bowl to Sun's home, but the door was closed. I called her name. Sun opened the door to let me in. Oh, it was dinner time here too. Ahn welcomed me warmly to join them.

They also had fried bamboo shoots, but not as delicious as my Mom's. Perhaps Jing had never cooked it before. Sun tasted a piece of my bamboo shoots.

"Yours tastes better," she said.

I was surprised to see that Ahn had not only shaven his beard, but also dressed in his suit like before. Now he was just as I always remembered him - he looked like a teacher again.

While most of his teaching colleagues dressed in Chinese tunic suits Ahn had always chosen to wear western style suits. It set him apart from the others and they used to tease him about it, saying it was because his wife was a tailor.

Privately, I thought it was the styles he'd seen overseas that influenced his choice of clothes.

After dinner, Sun and I chatted in her bedroom. She told me that Ahn had come home because of the festival for the Beginning of Winter, an important traditional Chinese celebration.

Later I remembered how excited Ahn had seemed that night. He kept talking, joking with everyone, including me, as though he had not been allowed to speak for many years and now he wanted to pour out all the words he had stored in his heart, while he had the chance.

After Ahn returned to the Cadre School, Sun told me some of the things he had experienced there, but she stressed that Ahn had probably not told her everything.

After arriving at the Cadre School, Ahn was trained into strict routines. The students were all thought-criminals and were subjected to serious rules, doing heavy physical labor, learning the quotations of Chairman Mao and Marxism-Leninism, re-training themselves as farmers.

"I am no longer miserable there," he said to Sun.

"How can that be?"

"I am so tired every day, I sleep like a dead pig," he laughed, "And I'm good at feeding pigs now too."

Ahn had joked about his new life as he talked to Sun about it. Now she imitated his tone in describing it to me and was able to laugh about it herself. But now and then she would stop laughing and stare into space, seeing something that wasn't there.

"He so loved his teaching, and his fishing, but now..."

"Couldn't he take his fishing gear with him?" I asked.

Sun sighed sadly. "He's not allowed," she said.

I was silent for a while, trying to think of a way to comfort her. I looked up and the cloudy sky gave me inspiration.

"The best fishing season is over now anyway," I said.

Sun said nothing, but she too stared up at the grey clouds.

Chapter 13

There was a crowd around the bulletin wall.

I walked close to see what was going on. But, my view was blocked by taller bodies, so I squeezed between them until I was close enough to read the posters displayed there. Everyone was discussing them.

One of the revolutionary model dramas, called The Red Detachment of Women would be shown tonight. This was something to look forward to. I was so excited, I wanted to pee.

At that time, movies and revolutionary model dramas, were big events for everyone, especially children, because our town was so isolated by the mountains around, our daily life seemed boring and dreary compared to these glimpses of life beyond them.

We all enjoyed the rare sense of escape from our physical barriers that they gave us, as we imagined ourselves in touch with the outside world, however briefly.

I told Sun the news. It made her happy. She loved performing in plays and had told me of her dream of becoming an actress. Except for fashion design, no other dream meant so much to her.

"I like to dress in colorful costumes," she said. "I could live so many lives, through acting. I could become anyone!"

I waited impatiently all day. Time passed too slowly. Would evening never come? When Mother came home at last, I asked her to cook earlier.

"Why?" she said.

"I want to go to the opera with my friends."

Mother hesitated, and then she insisted that children should go with their parents. But I wanted the fun of going with friends my own age, especially Sun.

"Why can't I go with my friends?"

"It's too dangerous. There are crowds"

"That's the best part!"

"I don't understand you."

"You don't need to understand."

"I'm hungry now, Mother!"

"Why so much earlier than usual?"

"I'm a child, small belly."

She couldn't help smiling at that. Then she sighed and started to cook. Father was too busy at the desk writing his posters and he ignored our discussion. He had no interest in movies or revolutionary model dramas.

I ate so fast, I almost choked several times. Mother tried to reassure me.

"Slow down - you have plenty of time."

Father sent me serious glances but said nothing. My brother and sister just bowed their heads to their food. They ate quickly, too.

After dinner, I gulped down a bowl of water and slipped outside. Mother began to speak, but to my relief she stopped and just sighed. I ran to

Sun's home as fast as I could.

I arrived just as Sun finished her dinner, but, Jing would not allow her to go with me alone, so I lied, saying my family would be there. Jing let her go with me.

We hurried up to the school campus. It was crowded and noisy. Everything was brightly lit, especially the stage, which was almost as bright as daylight. Sun and I squeezed our way through the crowds towards the stage and waited for the curtain to open.

We sat close to the stage. It suddenly reminded me of the last time I had been at this spot, on the day of the "Five Types of People." The memories made me feel strange.

But all those worries vanished when the curtains opened at last. Music rose up. Actors and actresses appeared onstage, and the drama began.

I whispered to Sun, "Their cheeks and lips are so red!"

In our daily life, no one wore make-up, except perhaps Sun's own family.

"They must use it," she explained softly, "so the emotions on their faces can show up clearly, even under the strong lights.

The Red Detachment of Women was a sad and popular revolutionary model drama. The story was about a woman from the countryside called Ms. Wu Qionghua who was assaulted by her landlord.

Mr. Hong Changqing, the representative of the underground party, inspired her to join the Red Army and fight for her freedom. In the end, she inspired more women to join up and fight against landlords.

Apart from Mr. Hong, their party representative, Ms. Wu's team members were all women, so they became known as The Red Detachment of Women. There were many bloody scenes. The main actors were tortured and assaulted by their enemy, but Ms. Wu and Mr. Hong, did not surrender.

In one scene Mr. Hong, was caught by the Security Mission and burnt to death, but his courage in the face of death only inspired the country-women who all then joined the Red Army to resist the landlords.

The performance enthralled us. It was like a hallucination, a hint of all the possibilities of the wide world that existed beyond our knowledge. We lost ourselves in the drama. We applauded the skill of the performers. But all too soon, the music stopped and the curtain came down, returning us to humdrum reality.

On our way home, Sun relived the plot, commenting on the performance and the stage properties. She criticized the costumes, insisting they could be improved a lot.

"They could have made better flames for the fire by using red cloth..." she said. "But those broadswords were horrible and the dancing was so powerful..."

I agreed with Sun about the broadswords. They scared me. When the women stretched them towards the audience and cut the air, I thought they would cut off our heads.

"But I like the Red Star they wear," I said, and I really did think those stars were awesome. I'd never had one but always wanted one.

Sun paid no attention to my words. She was still too excited and busy assessing the performance.

At that moment, I looked to the sky, suddenly remembering that Sun knew what she was talking about. She herself was an experienced performer, well-known and recognized for her own parts in school productions. I sighed slightly in the dark.

As we rounded the corner of the street approaching Sun's house, we almost collided with Moon in the darkness. We would have screamed with fright, but Moon put a finger to her lips to silence us.

Sun made faces to me, slipping inside the door.

"Good night!"

Chapter 14

After that night, Sun and Moon often discussed The Red Detachment of Women. Soon they were planning their own performance of the story. They recruited their sisters to perform alongside them. Sun offered me the role of Mr. Hong.

"You are the perfect person," she said.

"Wow, great!"

"Can you help us to prepare some props?"

"What do you need?"

"You're good at making toys - we need weapons for the play."

"No problem." I said. "It's my favorite job!"

I managed to contact Uncle Chen to bring pieces of bamboo. A few days later, he arrived carrying just what I needed. I worked hard, using a knife to carve the bamboo into the shape of broadswords.

I produced wonderful weapons for Sun, but I still did not like those broadswords so I cut a piece of wood to make a pistol for myself. It looked great. Soon everything was ready and all we had to do was find a suitable time and place to practice performing.

One day, Jing went to visit Ahn. The trip would take her all day. It was the chance we'd been waiting for. We tried to hide our excitement.

The performance was held in the sewing room. Being the only boy, I had to take the two opposing male parts of the heroic party representative Mr. Hong Changqing and the evil landlord Nan Batian. This presented difficulties. We skylarked and ruined our own work by laughing at unsuitable moments in the performance.

"One's the good guy; the other's the bad guy."

Somehow I had to flip-flop between the two in an instant. As the landlord, I had to stick moustaches in my face; but a moment later, as Mr. Hong, I had to tear them off again.

I hopped back and forth from one character to the other, switching props in a flash. I made so many mistakes, Sun and her sisters laughed themselves silly.

"Don't frown...you're a good guy!"

"Now you're the bad guy! You should not smile!"

"Hey! You forgot your moustaches!"

In one scene the landlord tied the party representative Mr. Hong to a big tree and burnt him to death. So, as the actor of both roles the plot required me to tie myself up and burn myself to death. It was impossible and ridiculous.

Sun and Moon also had to switch from being members of The Red Detachment of Women into members of the landlord's security panel. More laughter.

"My comrades become my enemies!"

It forced them to leap from costume to costume to act the opposing parts. They switched from colorful to dark, and then back again; or from female to male and back again. The chaos mounted. Costumes were lost among the mess we created. We wore garments that might better fit babies or giants and we wore things that were only half finished.

And yet, despite all the humor, our determination to take the play seriously never wavered. We tried not to laugh but we failed, and we argued and joked about make-up and costumes in spite of ourselves.

"If I were the landlord, I will marry all of you!" I said.

"How dare you..."

Then Sun and her sisters held up their broadswords as The Red Detachment of Women, and prepared to cut my head open. In mock terror, I ran away from their broadswords, screaming and racing through the house, upstairs and down.

"There is no escape," they bellowed. "Where you go, we follow."

They chased me everywhere and all of us laughed and screamed.

But the fun ended when Jing returned from the Cadre School earlier than expected and anxiously described Ahn's situation to his daughters.

"They're turning him into a farmer!"

When the faces of her daughters did not respond with the matching anxiety she expected, she picked up the excitement they could barely conceal and soon the mess in the house gave everything away. Once the truth was discovered she admonished them all.

"No more plays in the house."

"We're sorry. Next time we won't make a mess."

"There will be no next time!"

We were not allowed to do the play again in Sun's house, so we decided to do it secretly somewhere outside. One day, we excused ourselves and sneaked away to the river bank to practice, but conditions there were not ideal.

The wind was blowing hard, chilling our bodies, muffling our words and shaking the plants around us. And we had no changing room, so we could not practice our costume switches as we changed from one character to another.

However the bleak atmosphere at least matched parts of the plot, being so sad and gloomy. We worked on, in spite of the gloom. Part way through the performance Moon asked for a pee-break, so we all stopped to rest. She walked towards the nearby bushes.

Suddenly, she screamed and ran back to us.

A young man in uniform appeared from behind the bushes. He walked towards us; I grabbed my wooden pistol and Sun and her sisters raised their broadswords.

But he quickly reassured us that he was no threat and had been sitting there resting before we came.

"I hoped I have not disturbed your performance."

We all hesitated, wondering what to do, then Moon spoke to him.

"Who are you?"

"My name is Hong..."

"Mr. Hong..."

"No, it is my first name..."

"Oh, I thought ...the party representative Mr.Hong..."

"You like drama?"

"Yes."

"You are good at it."

We felt flattered, so we chatted a while with him. He told us he was the head of the army's troupe of actors and he suggested that Moon should consider joining the troupe.

"If it's what you want, I may be able help you!" he said to her.

When he walked away at last, Moon stood motionless and enraptured for several seconds before springing to life. Then she ran to catch up to him and the two of them talked together. She returned to us with bright eyes and shining face.

That night I was restless. In the morning I woke with a headache, a cough, a runny nose and a sore throat.

"How many times have I told you to dress warmer?' said Mother.

I detested wearing my dark ugly overcoat, though I dared not admit it to Mother.

"I thought I was warm enough," was all I could say.

Mother sighed and made ginger tea for me. It needed more sugar. Oh, how I missed Jing's fig syrup at that moment. It was so long since I'd tasted it.

But the ginger tea soon warmed and soothed me. I lay under my warm quilts, staring up at the mosquito net, dozing and dreaming.

Mother came home at lunch time and cooked rice gruel for me. There were pieces of pork in it. At that time, Mother was making use of her cooking skills to work as the chef at a bank, but sometimes she had to do other odd jobs to help our family.

After lunch, I went back to bed. Mother put her hand on my forehead to check my temperature, then she relaxed and seemed happier with my condition.

"I have to go out now,' she said. "I have to work at unloading cement packages. We must work hard to avoid becoming capitalist."

I did not understand.

"What is capitalist? What does it look like?"

It made no sense to me. But, Mother said no more. As usual she focused on the action, not the theory.

"You don't need to understand. Just watch the grown-ups and do as we do."

Chapter 15

Soon afterwards a rumor spread through the town. Something big had happened. Moon had been accepted into the army troupe. She was destined for the bright lights of the big city far away from us. The news was like a thunderbolt to everyone.

At that time, to be a soldier was the big dream for many, an honor not just to the soldier himself, but also to his or her family. Now Moon was to become a soldier! It seemed impossible, but it was true.

The story was whispered everywhere. Many were jealous of her success. What was so special about Moon that she should receive such an honor? What was her secret? We few children were the only ones who knew what had happened to her that day beside the river.

Moon had only told her family - she herself was not the one who leaked the secret. Shortly before she went away, she patted my head and encouraged me to eat more, grow up quickly, and make my own dreams come true.

'You can be the next successful one," she joked.

"My own dreams?" I mumbled.

At that moment, I saw how beautiful Moon was! Even though the sky was clouded, there was a light in her eyes, a glow on her pale face. It reflected the happiness she felt in her great stroke of luck. Her dreams were coming true.

Then, as we passed the bridge, she murmured softly to the air.

"I am to escape at last."

Her eyes followed the river downstream as I walked beside her. I was the only one who heard her say it. That word again. Escape!

It took me back to the day I had stood on top of the mountain looking down on the river and dreaming of my own escape.

Escaping what? I did not know. And how? I didn't know that either. My spirits fell. Perhaps my mother was right when she said I thought too much. But still, the future was a mystery where anything was possible.

On the day of Moon's departure, we crossed the bridge and arrived at the bus station. Jing spoke little, just exhorting Moon to look after herself. Sun and her sisters reminded Moon to write often.

"And send photos!" they begged.

We stood there chatting softly, waiting for the bus. Others hung about nearby, jealousy and confusion written on their faces as they tried to think of something to say. But in the end they said nothing and I wondered if that was because Ahn was still in the Cadre School.

The bus driver called the last passengers aboard. It was time for Moon to go. Jing passed a package to her, saying nothing. Moon entered the bus, the engine started and the bus pulled away.

Jing ran after the bus, waving to Moon. Moon turned back to wave to her family. I stood there, watching and waving as her beautiful face gradually disappeared into the dust.

All the way home, Sun walked in silence.

All of us felt the loss of Moon but her departure had positive effects.

Things improved for her family.

One afternoon, as I walked towards the town center, I encountered Ahn coming towards me on the bridge. His face was happy.

He did not speak to me - just walked quickly past, perhaps in too much hurry to notice me. I looked back as he passed and it seemed that he carried all his belongings, either on his back or in his hands.

That evening, I told Father and Mother that Ahn had returned. They looked at one another, saying nothing. But, Father seemed to relax a little, and he drank more than usual that night. Mother murmured occasionally. Was she speaking to herself or to the air?

Father looked at me.

"You can never tell what might happen," he said, "Will Ahn go back to school?"

I shook my head. Although I was a pupil, I did not know everything that happened in high school. Father realized that and turned his eyes to my brother.

"I've heard nothing about it either," he said.

Father became silent. He just sat drinking and eating, his face inscrutable, until dinner was over. Then he went to his room.

"More sleep. Less talk. That is safer!" he said as he shut the door.

Later, Sun told me that Ahn would soon be back at school. How could that be? No one knew the reason, not even Ahn himself. But, people guessed that it might be something to do with Moon becoming a revolutionary soldier. Then Sun quoted other comments that she'd heard about her father.

"They say that the Cadre School has only washed away the dirt from his skin but now he must work harder than before to clean the dirt from his mind."

"What dirt? How can he clean his mind?"

Those words confused us both. It seemed like some complicated adult theory that we were too young to understand.

But for a while after that, it was almost as though our old life had resumed.

The weather was cold and the sky often cloudy, so when the sun made a rare appearance, I would make the most of it by leaning on a sun-warmed wall and dreaming.

I played at Sun's house again, now that the atmosphere had relaxed. Jing told fairy tales to us again during her work breaks, and just like before we heard the sounds of Ahn reading his English texts or hammering away as he worked at his hobby in his workshop.

Sometimes, when Jing was especially busy, Ahn helped her like Moon used to. I thought of Moon sometimes, helping her mother, always with a tape measure hanging around her neck and sometimes a shell shaped chalk in her hand, marking and cutting the colored cloth and singing like a happy skylark. But now she was far away from us all.

Sometimes I was lucky enough to be allowed to watch Ahn working at his hobby. How I envied him his wonderful workshop, with all his tools spread around him, as he worked at making his fishhooks; beating and cutting and shaping the steel wires, and placing the many finished hooks into his store box.

"You are good at this job," I said. "Do you still go fishing?"

"Yes. But, now is not the best time."

"Oh?"

"It's better in summer."

Yes, I missed summer too, especially those long hot days when we cooled off by swimming in the river, something my Father did not permit. But he could not watch me all the time, so I swam when he was at work. His hours were longer than ever now because of the unpredictable meetings. The river was a wonderful playground.

"Would you like to learn English?" said Ahn suddenly.

I had never thought about it before. I could not answer at once. At that time, I still preferred playing to studying. I mumbled, but did not answer clearly. Ahn smiled and comforted me.

"It doesn't matter, maybe one day."

Ahn's face was darker than before he went away. Sun liked to play with his earlobe and tease him about his skin color. It made Ahn happy. He stopped working, and crawled on all fours like a horse, letting Sun ride on his back.

"Father, you look like a farmer now!"

I was a little shocked by Sun's behavior, but I envied her close relationship with her parents, especially her father. My own father never took time to have fun with his children - we saw only his serious side.

When she finished playing with Ahn, Sun told me that Moon had written to them. She reported details of Moon's daily life to me, her new routine of singing and rehearsing and performance and makeup. I was sorry Moon had not sent a photo. We both wanted to see how she looked now.

"She promised to include a photo next time," said Sun.

Chapter 16

At Chinese New Year Eve, Mother came home earlier than usual and cooked only rice. Then she boiled water, calling us to have a hot bath. We children dressed in new clothes while Mother washed the dirty clothes we'd taken off.

Meanwhile Father took over the cook's role in the kitchen. He killed a chicken for dinner, chopping the meat and vegetables into pieces, cooking and serving the food. He did it expertly, like a real chef, quicker than Mother.

As a Hakka guy, Father did not cook in everyday life, but took charge of the kitchen on festivals and special days, surprising us with his skill.

When he finished cooking, Father went for his own bath, emerging from the bathroom freshly shaved and looking younger than usual, dressed in a new Chinese tunic suit. He seemed happier than usual, and even a little tender towards us.

That night dinner was served early. Father tried to create a lighter atmosphere at the table, but he was not good at this. We were so accustomed to his usual sternness, we still felt the old authority around us and could not relax enough to laugh freely.

I ate quickly without words, and my sister and brother did also.

I finished eating and slipped out the door. I went to Sun's home. The family were having dinner. Ahn invited me to join them. It was not the custom to visit at mealtimes, but we children did not care about that.

I had already eaten so I declined his offer. As Sun was not free to come out and play, I returned home disappointed, to wait for the fireworks show without her.

Time dragged. The boredom made me sleepy. My eyelids drooped.

Explosions jolted me to full wakefulness. Firecrackers! Now was the time to farewell the old year and celebrate the new.

Excitement sent me rushing to join the crowds in the streets, hoping to find unexploded firecrackers on the ground, always a favorite activity on Chinese New Year Eve.

The gunpowder smell of the fireworks intoxicated me. I ran about in the dark, searching everywhere, snatching up any stray unspent ones I found on the ground and gleefully pocketing them.

The excitement climaxed when I made the mistake of placing a still-smoldering cracker in my pocket. It caused an explosion which blew my pocket to shreds.

The happiness continued in the morning. Father gave us luck-money wrapped in red paper- a New Year custom intended to make us both good and lucky in the future. I unwrapped mine and played with the pretty new banknote, enjoying its firmness and the crisp sounds that it made.

Meanwhile, Mother hand-stitched my shredded pocket, but I was dis-appointed with the ugly repair. I wondered if Jing might do a better job, so I went to Sun's house after breakfast.

Normally, people did not visit others on Chinese New Year's Day, but as usual, we children did as we pleased. Jing used her scissors and sewing machine to improve on Mother's repairs. It looked better, though still not as good as it was.

I told Sun about my evening among the firecrackers.

"It was exciting! I missed you. Where were you?"

"I stayed home. Father talked to us all night about his life at the Cadre School."

"Was it fun for him there?"

"No! He was not good at the work they gave him. He had never done it before."

"So he..."

"He did not like it, but he had to do it."

Sun was dressed in a green satin overcoat. The fabric was decorated with a white peony design and it shone with a rich gloss. A vision entered my head that this beautiful girl standing here in the real world would be perfect to take the role of the landlord's daughter in a movie.

But her eyes were sad as she continued Ahn's story.

"He had no chance to wear his suit in there. They made him dress like a farmer. When the real farmers found out he could speak English, they laughed at him."

"Why?"

"They say it's birds' language."

"Can that be true?"

"Father is missing Christmas now."

Suddenly, Sun began talking about Christmas, the biggest festival of the year in Western culture, so different from our Chinese New Year's celebrations.

We remembered Christmas fairy tales that Jing had told us. In those stories feathery snow fell from the sky, casting enchantment over the land, the trees, the streets, houses and castle towers.

"A white world!"

"A cold world!"

I liked that kind of fairy tale.

Most stories had a princess, perhaps living in a castle with bright candles and great feasts. Perhaps she would go outside to pick mushrooms and become lost in the snowy wilderness, only to be found and rescued by her handsome prince.

"It's a shame our festival is not in winter," I said.

"Why?"

"There is no snow for our New Year."

Sun burst the bubble of my imagination by explaining that her parents were born in Indonesia where Christmas was never cold and snowy.

"A Christmas without snow? What did they eat?"

"Turkey."

"What's turkey?"

Sun was born in China. She herself had never seen or tasted turkey, so she could only repeat what she'd heard from her parents. She did her best to explain what a turkey looked like, but it wasn't easy for her.

She reminded me that Jing had mentioned them in some of her fairy tales. But I had never even seen a picture, so I was still confused.

"It looks like a chicken but way bigger."

"What shape? What color?"

"I don't know. I've never seen one either, but Father promised to take us to celebrate Christmas with snow one day."

"Wow!"

Suddenly she changed the subject, "Moon sent us two pictures!"

She showed me both, one of Moon in army uniform and the other wearing stage costume and make-up, and looking like a new kind beauty- a mixture of charm and heroic spirit.

Rumors continued to circulate in the town that Ahn's release from the Cadre School was because Moon was an actress of the army troupe. This gave her family the protection of someone in power.

Was it true or false? I did not know. I only knew that when Ahn was home, his family was happy, especially Sun. When Sun is happy, I am too, I thought.

I liked his reading and hammering. It meant I could again enjoy the colorful world of his household.

Chapter 17

After Chinese New Year, the weather gradually improved, but sometimes the chill returned as though winter wanted to stay. I was not allowed to take my overcoat off.

"No more colds!" warned Mother.

At that time, Mother and Father became busier, because our world was quickly changing. No one knew what would happen next, but everyone went along with the flow, following the orders and guides that came down through the ranks from the highest levels.

Chairman Mao wanted China to grow strong and powerful, to catch up with Britain and the USA as soon as possible. He wanted China to independently create iron and steel products. He expected everyone to help. It was a big new direction for our country.

My parents discussed it over dinner.

"How can we produce iron and steel here?'

"We just do it."

"But, we are not steelworkers."

"No problem, we are Chinese people!"

I did not understand, but we children were happy because the new steelworks construction site became another playground for us. We went there often to watch the grown-ups.

Thousands of people responded to the call of Chairman Mao to work hard together. They all crowded to the scene. Red flags waved everywhere in the wind. Oh, what a spectacle it was!

Propaganda teams beat their noisy drums and gongs, shouting Revolutionary Slogans and singing the Red Revolutionary Songs, encouraging people to work harder and harder.

People learned quickly, copying the design drawings fed to them by the authorities. Soon they were building the furnaces.

Even teachers and older students came to help. They were happy to begin with, digging the earth, helping to transport the cement and bricks and other building materials. They all worked with passion.

With everyone working so hard, day and night, the new industry quickly took shape before our amazed eyes. The chimneys grew up and up towards the sky, like giant sprouting bamboo shoots.

I had seen documentaries showing the same thing happening in other towns. Now we were a part of the great new story being created in China. We children hung around to enjoy the action and excitement.

People loaded and unloaded coal, firewood and scraps of iron and all were sent into the furnaces.

The leader of the workers shouted at us. "You kids get out of here! This is a workplace, not a playground!"

But the children only crowded closer, shouting and laughing, feeling the heat from the furnace. They tried to drive us away but we always sneaked back again. It was a kind of hide-and-seek game we played with the adults.

Sun's mother worked there too. But she was not good at the job and made too many mistakes. Others were dissatisfied with her and they whispered their complaints behind her back.

"That clumsy woman!"

"Look at her clothes! She does not wear overalls."

Yes, Jing's silk overcoat made her conspicuous among the working people. But, no one criticized her openly, perhaps because they remembered that her daughter Moon was in the army.

Sometimes, I sat on a low wall not far from the furnace site, watching the crowds and the action and hearing the Revolutionary Songs echoing down the wind from the loud-speakers. Heavy smoke rose from the chimneys and disappeared into the sky.

Suddenly, Sun arrived beside me.

"My clothes got dirty," she complained.

Her white peony flowers were stained.

"Don't worry, I said. "The weather's getting warmer. You won't need an overcoat soon."

"What would you know, dirty boy!"

Sun giggled and pointed at me. I tried to tidy myself with my hands but my dirty fingers only made it worse.

Sun laughed aloud.

"What's that on your face? Is it coal? Or ashes?"

We ran home and both of us laughed at our dirty reflections in the mirror.

As the days passed and the work never stopped, many soon tired of it, especially those who were not suited to the heavy physical labor, like the teachers and students. But still, nobody would complain publicly.

"We look like muddy monkeys!" was all they dared to say, or, "My new clothes are ruined!"

Every day, my brother and sister came home exhausted and filthy. The only time they could complain was when they were safe at home, but no one could get out of doing their share - the mission was compulsory, by order of the authorities.

At the same time, we all had to comply with a new order. People were now required to hand over almost all of their iron and steel possessions like pots and pans, tools, ploughshares, iron hoes, etc. All these items were collected together, then sent into the furnaces, to make new iron and steel products.

"But how can we cook without pots?" said Mother.

"Don't worry about it," said Dad.

"But we have to eat!"

"The Party will handle it."

Most days, Father and Mother were very tired after working so hard, but they were excited to be summoned to the city council building, which we now called the People's Commune.

Thousands of townspeople now gathered there daily. The building became one big restaurant for the people - a crowded and noisy place!

It was the biggest restaurant I had ever seen. Great washbasins filled with many different meats and vegetables, all heaped up like small hills on the tables. People sat there under the light bulbs, drinking and eating and chatting.

Never had I seen such a feast!

My mouth watered as I rushed to join the crowds. The most wonderful thing was not just the quality of the food, but permission to eat as much as we wanted. For the first time in our lives I was allowed to eat until I could eat no more.

I remembered my father's words, "The Party will handle it."Now I understood his meaning.

I ate. Then I ate more and more again. I kept eating until I could not hold another bite. When I finished at last, I had eaten so much it was hard to stand up and I stumbled away with difficulty from that crowded and noisy feast.

I found Sun outside and she was happy too. We shared stories of what we had eaten and laughed about the tightness of our bellies as we walked towards home, chatting and joking all the way.

On the way I met my Grandparents. Grandma was guiding Grandpa along his path but he seemed a little drunk and was singing softly.

'How are you feeling Grandpa?" I asked.

He smiled and murmured to the air, or maybe to me.

"My thanks to the Party!" he said.

"Thanks to Chairman Mao!" I agreed.

"We are becoming a true communist society!"

"And everything is free!" I said

"May it continue at least until I die!" he muttered.

"What does that mean?"

"You do not need to know. Just eat while you can. Enjoy the communist society!"

That night no-one slept well. We had all eaten too much. I tossed in my bed, gazing up at the mosquito net, wondering what the table might hold tomorrow.

Then the school notified us that all the students and teachers must go to the mountains to collect firewood to feed the furnace.

We did not like this commission, but, we could not complain in public.

"Physical exercise is good for you," said Mother. "It makes your body healthy. And remember there's a big feast afterwards."

I was annoyed to have to spend my time working but my Grandma went with us, so I distracted myself by talking to her as we walked towards the mountains. It was great consolation to discuss our big restaurant.

"Grandma?"

"Well?"

"What will be on the table tonight?"

"Perhaps pork meat and radish."

"How about fried bacon with spring bamboo shoots?"

"Both are good," she smiled.

After we arrived, I was cheered to see bamboo shoots shooting up from the ground everywhere in the forest, like green bullets frozen in flight as they shot half way out of the earth.

I remembered my Uncle Chen bringing us bamboo shoots in season and the wonderful meals my mother made from them. But Grandma would not let me pick any.

"Why not?" I asked. "They're wonderful food."

I knew Grandma agreed, but she would not change her mind. What was wrong with her?

"Why not? It's a waste not to take any."

"Now we all eat in the Restaurant of the People's Commune, we are not allowed to store food privately at home anymore," she explained.

"But we can keep it secret," I said.

"Ah, you are only a child!"

She would say no more about it. We began our work in the forest, going here and there gathering firewood. I puzzled about it as I worked, but I found no satisfactory answer.

At last it was time to hit the road for home. When I lagged behind in my tiredness, Grandma knew the best way to encourage me.

"Hurry up! Delicious food is waiting for us!"

It worked. Suddenly I was starving, and I walked faster.

We arrived at last, unloaded the firewood, and hurried to the Restaurant of the People's Commune. Wow! It was so good to be eating again. Once again I ate until I could hold no more.

As we stumbled home after dinner, someone mentioned Fatty's father Lee.

"Lee's been caught by the militias."

"Why is that?"

"He tried to hide some beans at home secretly."

"That son of a bitch!"

Chapter 18

Now that people all ate together in the Restaurant of the People's Commune, residents no longer cooked at home. No one was allowed to store or hide food stuff privately, so Lee had made a big mistake.

For years he had enjoyed chewing fried beans, not only at dinner while drinking, but also in the daytime. But Lee took advantage of his position as one of the chefs at the Restaurant of the People's Commune.

One early morning, he was making tofu from soya beans. The tofu was to be sent to the mill to become soy milk. Perhaps he enjoyed too much the golden color and good smell rolling in his palms.

His mouth must have watered as he worked until he could not resist putting some beans into his pockets. No doubt he got away with it several times.

But he was reported in the end by an alert chef, who took the militias to raid Lee's home. They arrived suddenly, asking Lee to confess his crime and hand over the stolen beans. The chef stayed there watching what happened and he reported everything he saw into the town's gossip.

Lee panicked at first, and denied the accusation. He declared his innocence. So the militias searched every corner of his house. Finally, they found a bottle with beans inside it, buried under his house.

"Explain this." said the militias and their tone was serious as they shook the bottle in his face. Lee heard the sounds made by the beans inside the bottle. He had no answer for them, so he bowed his head and his face turned pale.

His colleagues accused him in the assembly; people were angry and went up to the stage to report Lee's crimes.

"He tried to persuade me to do the same."

"He tried to bribe me!"

"He did this."

"He did that."

Someone also exposed Lee for stealing dog meat from the dog hunting team. My God! So many of his crimes were uncovered at that assembly.

"Son of bitch!"

Lee kept his head down, bearing the accusation of the crowds. I felt vindicated because I remembered what the dog hunting team had done to Prince. They all should go to hell, I thought. I raised my fist, and joined with the crowd to shout popular slogans against Lee.

"He would starve us to death!"

"He stole our food!"

"He should go to hell!"

"Make an example of him!"

The angry echoes were so loud, they filled the meeting place and far beyond it. Lee's body continued to shake until the militias took him away. The assembly moved on to the next item on the agenda.

I saw Uncle Chen walk up onto the stage with red flowers on his chest;

several farmers accompanied him to set up a big display board, using pictures to show the success of the rice harvest.

Uncle Chen proudly announced how the production team of his village had improved on their output of grains. Their yield was now far larger than before.

Uncle Chen was so proud, he grabbed the microphone, urging all the farmers to stand tall and take pride in their huge harvest. The audience responded with explosive applause - thousands of people shouted and clapped, going crazy over him.

As Uncle Chen walked down from the stage he was surrounded by farmers with banners, all drumming and singing and shouting popular slogans, as they paraded towards the town center.

On my way home, I talked to Sun about what had happened to Lee.

"It was retribution for Prince."

Sun said nothing, just sighed deeply.

I felt a little dull, so I took out my candy wrapper to play with, folding and unfolding it.

It seemed so long since I had tasted candy. This wrapper was like a memento with its picture of the big white rabbit and his big buck teeth. I stared at it, remembering the wonderful sweetness and I also remembered the long-lost taste of fig syrup. Sun watched me closely.

"Close your eyes!" she said suddenly.

"Why?"

"Just close your eyes. Magic time!"

"Okay."

It did not feel like the right time to play hide and seek. What was Sun up to? But I closed my eyes and waited obediently. When I opened them there was a candy in her palm! It had a colorful wrapper.

"Wow! Where did you get it?"

"My relatives mailed it to us from overseas."

I did not know what to say, but my mouth watered. Sun put the candy into my palm. I unwrapped it, put it into my mouth, and the beautiful sweetness reached through my tongue, my throat, and flew straight to my heart.

Afterwards I studied the wrapper closely. There was writing on it and the picture of a dog. I did not understand the foreign lettering. But that cute dog looked so happy holding several colorful balloons in his forepaw.

I treasured that wrapper. I flattened and refolded it, placing it in my pocket. Many years later, I would learn that the dog was the famous Snoopy. But, at that moment, he just reminded me of Prince.

Chapter 19

One evening, Father brought a mousetrap home after work. It was made of wires, like a small cage. After dinner, Father held a family meeting to inform us of the latest directive from Chairman Mao. "Four Pests" had been defined and they must be wiped out in our country. They were fly, mosquito, mouse and sparrow.

"Why?"

"Not only bad people must be eradicated from our society, but also pests in nature. We will build a pure clean world."

"Pure clean world? How can that be?"

My brother replied before Mother had a chance.

"You are just a silly boy. The pests spread viruses and steal our grains."

There was something I did not understand. "Why would a mouse enter this trap?" I said.

My brother thought of himself as adult who could answer any question of mine. But, no one could answer that one, and all soon recognized the problem.

Next day, Father brought a small paper bag home.

"This is a special ration that is only to be used as bait," he explained.

There were beans inside the bag. Father put them into a bottle. Then he fixed a bean inside the mousetrap and set it at the corner of the kitchen. Next morning, there was a big ugly rat inside the mousetrap.

"It worked!"

The rat was panicking, running here and there inside the mousetrap, baring his sharp teeth at us. Father boiled the kettle in the kitchen, then poured the boiling water onto the rat.

The rat screamed. It scratched at the trap, trying to avoid the boiling water, and escape from the trap, but there was no way out. That terrible shrill screaming continued for far too long before it died in the end.

Boiling water was not the only way to kill vermin. Fire was often used too. Some people, especially children, liked to pour kerosene onto a rat's body, then light it.

Burning rats screamed as they ran here and there and rolled on the ground in a fireball. People yelled and chased them. Some thought it was fun, but the risks were great and the practice caused several fire accidents in the town.

Every day, almost every moment, the horrible screams were bursting out around the town. They made my hair stand on end. People were excited in public but, privately fearful.

My dreams turned to nightmares of mice screaming, scratching and escaping. Burning rats chased me through my dreams until I woke suddenly covered in sweat.

People had to hand in the tails of the rats to their units, so officials could count and report their achievements to headquarters. There was no requirement to pass the dead bodies to the Restaurant of the People's Commune. So when the screaming stopped, the people could feast.

Father removed the tails, and Mother cooked the meat for us. First she would burn off the coat of the mouse, then cut it up and wash it, before barbecuing it. It smelled good and the taste made us happy.

"But I miss my good tools," said Mother.

Most of our iron kitchen tools had been sent to the furnaces to make iron products. Now we only had things made from bamboo - items like bamboo bowls. If only Mother had proper kitchen tools, she could use better recipes.

Sun would not eat mouse meat. She said it made her sick. I tried to persuade her to just taste some, but she always flatly refused.

"It's hideous!"

"No, it's not. It's yummy!"

At that time, people killed and ate not only mice, but sparrows. Sparrows also tasted good and they were among the "Four Pests" we must eradicate. We climbed up trees and buildings, and removed all the eggs from their nests.

The people tried a new method to catch sparrows. We took dishes or washbasins or anything that could be beaten to produce a loud noise. The noise sent the birds into the air, but when they tried to find a place to land the same noise was going up everywhere.

Not only sparrows, but all kinds of birds, had to stay in flight above the town until they fell exhausted to the ground or onto the roofs of houses, where they were netted and killed.

What an uproar it caused in our town! Shouting and drumming and beating everywhere, day and night. But with all that hard work, the method worked well and the system quickly spread through the rest of the country.

Everyone was tired but proud of their success. The reward was the feast that followed. We gave only the legs of sparrows to the authorities, and barbecued the rest.

But, Sun would not eat bird meat either.

"But why not? It's so yummy!"

"It's too cruel and bloodthirsty."

Most of us thought she was just being conceited. Why shouldn't we enjoy the wonderful taste? Our mouths watered as we compared recipes.

Neither Sun nor Ahn enjoyed this food. But Ahn must be seen to support the campaign. He was good at making fishing tools, so he handed out fishing nets to help catch birds.

Every time, he was rationed sparrows or other kinds of birds, he gave them to his colleagues, saying he had no appetite. His colleagues were happy to receive them.

The campaign was a Mass Movement, the most excellent catchers would go to the meeting to share skills and experiences, so everyone could learn better ways to kill the "Four Pests".

Success came quickly. Almost all flies and mosquitoes were gone from the town; and all the mice and birds had gone into our mouths, through our bodies, and out the other end.

One morning, I woke up to an eerie silence; the absence of birdsong. All my life until then I had woken to the racket of birds outside.

But now, it was so quiet, I wondered if the people had disappeared too. Was it because it was Saturday? I got up to see what was going on outside. After breakfast, Mother told me the truth.

"They have gone!"

"What?"

"Not just sparrows, but all birds!"

Oh, yes, they all had gone! They had gone into our bellies.

I did not miss the flies and mosquitoes, but I missed the mice and birds. Yes, they tasted good, but we had enjoyed the taste too much, and must now live without the song. We could not have both.

Then a new directive came from Chairman Mao. If sparrows were too hard to find, people must kill cockroaches. And nowhere could we see a single bird.

Then we heard that Lee had been denounced as a saboteur because he fried and chewed the bait-beans. After he was fined by the Restaurant of the People's Commune, he could not take advantage of his position there anymore. He missed the fried beans so much he could not help himself.

"Those beans were only for baits."

"He is a saboteur!"

Because Lee's tally of killed mice was low, some officials already doubted that he worked as hard as others. But always Lee denied this accusation.

Then one day Lee came home and chatted to a neighbor at his gateway. They discussed the mouse-hunting campaign, sharing experiences and skills.

But the neighbor noticed a smell of fried beans in the air and grew curious. He looked around and spotted several fried beans which had dropped to the ground from a hole in one of Lee's trouser pockets. The story went public.

Once again Lee was subjected to criticism at the general assembly. When the story of the hole in his pocket was described, even his wife was labeled a lazy woman. Some wondered why he put beans into his pocket at all. Why not just eat them secretly at home.

"It's so stupid. Mouse meat is tastier than beans."

"Perhaps he just prefers fried beans to mouse meat."

"Maybe he's so greedy, he wants both."

"He's a rat!"

There were so many criticisms and comments, but Lee dared not try to defend himself, in case it drew more censure down upon him. There was nothing he could do but bow down his head and bear the abuse.

Chapter 20

At first it was only the taste of the bird meat that I missed from my daily life, because I hungered for a food that was gone. But later, my heart sensed the emptiness of a world without birdsong, and the silence intensified.

I remembered the birds perching on rooftops, or branches, hopping on the ground, foraging and singing. They were everywhere once.

But now, when I looked up to the rooftops or into the trees, there was nothing but a memory. Would I ever see them again?

But worse still, soon afterwards, the trees themselves disappeared. There was not enough coal to supply the furnaces and the furnaces must be kept burning. People had to cut down the trees to feed the flames.

Trees that once shaded the streets and the riverbanks, including the willow tree where Ahn loved to fish, all were cut down and sent into the fire, until none remained in the town.

I missed the trees, especially those in our school campus, in summer-time, which grew so tall and wide, like huge umbrellas sheltering the birds that twittered and sang among their leaves and branches. Those trees were the essence of summer!

But, now that the birds and the trees had disappeared, people could only sigh over the memories and try to comfort themselves.

"Maybe we can plant them again one day..."

But- we could only wait for the latest high guides that came from Chairman Mao, so far away in our great capital, Beijing city.

But- the lack of trees created an urgent problem. We now had to go further afield and spend more time to collect enough firewood to feed the furnaces. We looked to the mountains.

"Might there be birds hiding in the mountains?"

Anxious to find the answer I suddenly desired to go there with Grandma. Unfortunately, when we arrived, the few birds we did hear, all stayed out of sight.

"They are scared of us."

At that time we encountered many others on the road or in the mountains, all coming for the same reason. The mountains were no longer quiet. People sought fuel everywhere, even in the mountains.

Unfortunately, I broke my ankle on the journey home and I cried with the pain, until I realized the futility of tears out here in the wild.

I could not continue gathering fuel and nor could Grandma, because now she had to carry me home on her back. I felt guilty and apologized to her. But Grandma gave me no blame - only words of comfort.

"Oh, sweet heart, don't worry."

She even joked with me.

"You are more important than firewood!"

I would have laughed if not for the pain. When she stopped for her first rest, I tried again to walk by myself but it was impossible.

As she walked, my head rested on Grandma's shoulders. I could feel her sweat and hear her heavy breathing. I had never been so close to her as I was that day.

That journey seemed longer than any before. So many things were different; the pain, the sweat, the breathing. Even the clouds, the sky, the mountains, and the wind, seemed changed.

I arrived home at last. When my parents saw my ankle, they were scared.

They took me to the hospital doctor but the pain and heat continued in my broken ankle. It stopped me from sleeping at night. My mom was anxious, and always checking me, but she could do nothing to help.

The next few days, I had to stay at home all the time. It was boring and too quiet, with nothing to listen to, except the distant sound of someone shouting slogans somewhere in our town.

I had nothing to do but play endlessly with the candy wrapper that Sun had given me. Dad gave me comic books to look at, but they did not interest me.

Sometimes Sun came to visit me and brought outside news. Her parents were ill from the hard physical labor. They were not good at the work, but could not escape it. Worse, others complained they were causing delays.

Sun changed the subject to speak of Moon. "She travels a lot and performs in many places."

She showed me one of Moon's performance photos. I thought Moon looked so cool in her army uniform with her ears showing through her short haircut.

"When can she come home to visit?"

"Not sure. She's so busy travelling around the country."

"One day maybe we can be like her. Would you like that?"

Sun just smiled and did not reply.

"Is Jing telling fairy tales again?"

"No."

"Why?"

"She is too exhausted after her hard work."

"But..."

"Mother still has all her sewing to do. She spends every moment catching up on it."

When Sun left, Uncle Chen arrived to visit. This time, he brought no gift and he seemed exhausted. Because of my broken ankle, I could not stand to greet him.

"Please forgive me," I said.

"Never mind. I understand."

Uncle Chen came close and bent over me, checking my broken ankle. He pressed and pinched it gently with his fingers, asking what I felt at each touch. His next words offered me some hope of comfort.

"Next time I will bring you traditional Chinese medicinal herbs. It always works."

Uncle Chen walked to the corner of the living room, poured a bamboo cup of water from the bamboo kettle, and drank it dry. Then, he sat and waited anxiously for my parents. There was only silence in the house.

Chapter 21

Mother arrived first and began to cook for us in the kitchen. When Father came home soon after, he chatted with Uncle Chen in the living room. I moved carefully from my bed to the bamboo sofa and listened to them talking.

I sensed misunderstandings in their conversation. Uncle Chen seemed embarrassed as though there was something he needed to say but he could not bring himself to say it. Mother finished in the kitchen and called us to lunch.

When Father gave Uncle Chen some rice wine with his food, the alcohol gave him the courage to speak at last. Uncle Chen raised up his head, and without meeting my father's eye, he asked to borrow rice for his family.

"Borrow rice?"

My parents could not respond at once. His request confused them because we all remembered Uncle Chen and his villagers at the assembly reporting their huge harvest.

We'd all been there and heard his presentation about their great achievements. I was as confused as my parents. We stared at him in surprise and my parents seemed concerned and worried for him. Uncle Chen blushed in deep embarrassment.

Father spoke first.

"What happened?"

Uncle Chen did not answer at once, just bowed his head and sipped his rice wine in silence. His face was redder than before, so Father stopped drinking and questioned him again.

"Please say something!"

Father waited again for an answer. Uncle Chen sighed deeply and drank one more cup of rice wine. Then he seemed ready to take the plunge at last. He mumbled a little at first and then said something about lying.

"Speak more clearly," said Father. "Lying about what?"

It took Uncle Chen all his strength to reply and he spoke with his head bowed and his face reddened by both alcohol and shame.

"We did not have a big harvest!"

"That's not what you said at the assembly."

"We lied. Actually the harvest was terrible."

At that moment, Uncle Chen neither ate nor drank. He just sat there trembling slightly.

The truth shocked my parents. They didn't know what to say because clearly there was more to this situation than they yet understood.

My dad glanced at us, his children. His face was grave.

"Focus on your meal!"

We ate quickly. After lunch, my brother and sister slipped outside. Mum helped me back to my bedroom. But from my bed, because of the quietness inside the house, I still could hear something of their conversation. Although Uncle Chen and my dad spoke in low voices, I caught just enough to understand them.

Uncle Chen's village had hardly harvested anything. It was all a false boast.

"It is... the worst year!"

"Why ?"

"With all the birds gone, pests ran rampant. Reduced the harvest."

"But, why lie about it?"

"Everyone did so... I had to do it, too."

"Had to...?"

"They ... er ... encouraged us to lie."

"But you should not...Oh ... I think I understand. Ok, that is no problem."

At that time, the Restaurant of the People's Commune had collapsed, because it could not sustain the thousands of mouths of the people. Thousands of mouths! They had eaten the great grain mountains to almost empty. Everyone missed the bountiful past days, especially we children. But now it was no more than an amazing memory.

People were expected to cook individually at home, as of old.

Residents in the town were lucky. We were rationed by the authorities. For a while, every adult had 29 kilograms of rice monthly. But the size of each share soon came down.

The farmers did not have this advantage. They had to work hard in the fields and hand in most of their grain to the authorities, leaving only inadequate leftovers for themselves.

So, there was a problem for the farmers, if they boasted too much, they had to hand in more grain to the authorities. That meant they had less for themselves.

"We've almost run out of grain.

So I have to..."

I could hear Uncle Chen's sorrow and regret for what he had done. But, it was too late. Chinese people say that in all the world there is no medicine for regret. If you've done something wrong, you must pay for it one day.

I did not know how many kilograms of rice we loaned to Uncle Chen, I just knew that congee, the diluted rice-porridge, appeared more often on our table after his visit. But, my dad and mom did not complain.

"Friends should help each other."

Later, Uncle Chen came to visit us again. This time, he brought traditional Chinese medicinal herbs to cure my broken ankle. He opened a cloth bag, took out some herbs and showed my parents how to use them.

He went to the kitchen and used a knife to chop the herbs into pieces. Then he minced them to paste in a bowl. He spread them over my wounded ankle and wrapped it with a piece of cloth.

"It feels more comfortable already."

"You have to stay at home for one hundred days."

"Why so long?"

"One cannot do activities after serious injury to bones and muscles."

Uncle Chen told us that years ago he had learnt some theory of Chinese traditional medicine and physiotherapy from elderly people in his village. He explained the relevant details very carefully to my parents.

He would not relax until he was sure that my parents could handle my continued future treatment by themselves. Before leaving, he left a supply of the necessary herbs for my parents to use. Only then, did he take the road home.

His Chinese traditional medicine really worked, especially at night. I felt the heat in my broken ankle decrease at once and the pain gradually declined. At last I was able to sleep at night.

My parents kept up the treatment, day after day, exactly as Uncle Chen had taught them, but still it was months before I could walk outside by myself on my feet again freely. When the day came at last I was so happy.

For so long I had lain there, listening to sounds from outside and wondering what caused them. During that time, I could only rely on others to describe everything that happened around us. Now, the outdoors was like a new world waiting to be rediscovered.

I went to Sun's house, but the door was closed. I knocked, but no-one answered. I walked around the house and watched through the windows, but saw no-one inside.

Where were they all?

Then I walked to the town center. The atmosphere had changed somehow, though I could not easily describe it. I passed by the bulletin wall and saw names covered with red crosses.

I stepped closer. Words were still visible in the remaining corner of a torn paper. "Winter is passing away, spring is coming..." At that moment, several pedestrians passed by me in hurry.

I hung out in the town center until I felt hungry, then turned for home. I ate a bowl of gruel which helped a little. I complained to Mother that I always felt hungry now, with nothing but gruel to eat. She comforted me in a carefree tone.

"Eating lightly is better for your health..."

"But Mother it's not easy to be hungry!"

"You'll get used to it..."

Suddenly, I heard someone entering the house. I walked out of the kitchen. My brother was inside, searching stealthily for something he wanted to take.

"What are you doing?"

"None of your business."

"Are you looking for something?"

"No..."

"Why so sneaky then?"

"Advance the Revolution!" he said proudly, slipping outside again quickly.

Chapter 22

Uncle Chen arrived without warning. This time he carried no mountain products. He seemed exhausted and sweaty, but happy to see us again.

He asked me kindly about my broken ankle, "Are you better now?"

I told him I had already recovered completely. He let me sit on the bamboo sofa, and squatted in front of me to check my ankle. He squeezed it with his fingers, lightly at first and then more heavily.

"Any pain on this side?"

"No."

"Or on this side?"

"That's fine too."

"Recovered completely," I said again. "The traditional Chinese medicinal herbs really worked."

"We have used it for generations."

When he finished checking my ankle, Uncle Chen tried to stand, but he fell to the ground, and hurt his forehead. It scared us all. My parents helped him to his feet, and moved him carefully to a seat on the bamboo sofa.

"What's wrong with you?"

"A dizzy spell. That's all."

"Do you need a doctor?"

"Not at all. I'm just a bit hungry after my journey."

Father insisted Uncle Chen lie down on the sofa. Mother brought him a soft pillow and then went to the kitchen to cook. She worked quickly, and soon returned with a bowl of gruel for Uncle Chen.

Uncle Chen's eyes shone at the sight of it. He stopped breathing and struggled to sit up to take the bowl. But he was too eager to swallow it, and it scalded him. He had to stop, and blow on the gruel to cool it, spinning the bowl and sucking the food into his mouth carefully.

Uncle Chen emptied the bowl very quickly and then took a deep breath. We hoped it had not harmed him to eat so quickly. But, he looked a bit better than before. His eyes stayed fixed on the empty bowl. Mother glanced at Father and then served one more bowl for Uncle Chen.

"Why?" said Father.

Uncle Chen did not answer. After he finished the second bowl of gruel, he was like someone resurrected from near death, breathing deeply, sweating and trying to calm himself.

"We have nothing left!" he admitted.

He became vacant for several seconds, then breathed deeply and explained that his family had suffered hunger for some time now. The news shocked my parents. There was silence in the room. Then Father spoke slowly, one word at a time to ask Uncle Chena question.

"Have you reported this to the general secretary of the People's Commune?"

"Yes," replied Uncle Chen.

He then explained that the authorities had only insisted they must help themselves, and solve their problems by self-reliance. Uncle Chen's voice faded, and it seemed he wanted to cry.

"But we cannot!"

"Why not?"

"We have no spare plots for our own use. We can do nothing!"

"Don't worry. You can take rice from us."

Uncle Chen found it difficult to respond.

"...You are..."

My parents gave Uncle Chen a small bag of rice to take away. He thanked us with many tears and much gratitude. I had never seen a grown man cry like that before and it frightened me. I drummed my chest with my fists and went outside to find fresh air.

I walked to the town center and hung out there. I encountered a beggar in ragged clothes. He was holding an empty bowl and begging for food or money. He approached people, displaying his empty bowl to everyone.

"Give me a little..."

He won no sympathy. Most rejected him and walked away in disgust. Children followed him about, teasing him loudly.

The beggar began to sing. It was a beggar's song, murmured sadly to himself, or to others, or to nobody at all. It reminded me of that other singer, the thief who was caught and beaten in our town so many months ago.

Someone might have reported the beggar, because soon afterwards the militias came to check on him. He showed them his proof paper. It was no more than a torn scrap with a red seal on it.

"We have nothing to eat..."

"What?"

"Begging is my only hope ..."

"You must get out of this town!"

"I..."

"Shame on you!"

The beggar pleaded with the crowds around him, but the militias interrupted him shouting rudely as they drove him away from the main street. Children chased the beggar to the outskirts of town.

A crowd formed to discuss a rumor, that someone had stolen grains from the grain storage of the People's Commune, so now the authorities had to guard it with militias all time.

I listened for a moment, then walked to the grain storage to see for myself. There was a big dog there. I was curious - I had not seen a dog for a long time.

Someone told me the dog belonged to the army; another said it was owned by relatives of the general secretary of the People's Commune who had lent it out as a guard dog.

Over the next few days, after the first beggar had gone, more beggars came to haunt our town. But the residents could do nothing to help them, because like everyone else in those times, they suffered from hunger themselves.

Rumors circulated, all concerning hunger or grain. Someone had tried to steal grain or they had gone to prison for attacking the grain storage; or the watchdog had bitten someone. etc.

At home, my parents occasionally discussed the rumors but so many were spreading and there was no way of knowing which were true and which were false. In the end we stopped talking about it, because even speech wasted too much energy.

One day, we were called to an assembly to criticize a chef of the Restaurant of the People's Commune. He was denounced for supplying a steamed roll to a woman in exchange for sex. The crowds criticize the chef furiously, attacking him with bricks and rocks.

"You son-of-a-bitch!"

"You turn hunger to your own pleasure!"

"You deserve death!"

In minutes, the chef was covered in blood. But, no one sympathized with him. Many were almost hungry enough to eat him. After the crowds dispersed, people felt anger at the chef all over again, because of the energy they had wasted shouting and beating him minutes before.

My classmate Fatty seemed happy. He admitted to being the one who had exposed the chef's secret. He said he'd watched the guy for days. The chef always came home with something in his pocket, then the woman slipped into his house at night. So Fatty guessed that something was going on in there.

"One steamed roll can save a life."

"So I reported to the militias... to catch them in bed..."

Suddenly, someone teased Fatty.

"Is that what your own father does too maybe?"

Everyone laughed.

Fatty feared for his father's reputation.

"That's impossible!"

But no one believed him.

"How would a child understand such things, unless he had seen it before?"

The crowds laughed loudly.

Fatty blushed at once and collided with me in his rush to escape. He panicked and ran away from the laughter that followed him. But the people stayed there and continued discussing Fatty's father Lee.

"Maybe he fucked lots of women?"

"Son of a bitch!"

"Maybe he gave them a whole chicken!"

"Remember when we all ate meat every day?"

I stood among the crowds and listened to those rumors and guesses, amazed at what they could dream up about Lee. Just thinking about the food made all of us hungry. There was a sudden angry shout from among the laughter.

"Fuck you all! Stop talking and laughing!"

"Why?"

"It's making me hungry!"

Things got worse.

A few days later, Uncle Chen visited again. We could hardly recognize him. His face was swollen with dropsy, his skin transparent. He looked like a stranger to us.

He almost fell while entering our home. Father assisted him to sit at first and then lay him down in the bamboo sofa. I noticed that Uncle Chen's hands seemed bigger than before. Wherever Father touched him, his fingers left deep impressions on Uncle Chen's skin.

My uncle seemed too exhausted to speak.

He closed his eyes and slept for a while, then struggled to wake up, trying weakly to speak to my parents.

"We have run out of grain . . . no more in store . . . eating tree bark . . . grass. . . roots. . . white clay."

He managed to describe how his people were eating anything they could find, just to fill their stomachs, until in the end it became difficult to defecate. Bellies became bloated until they looked like pregnant women.

"The people are beginning to die..."

Uncle Chen had no energy to cry, but I saw tears on his face. My parents had nothing to say. Silence spread through the room. Talk solved nothing. It was only a waste of energy.

Unfortunately, this time, Uncle Chen could not take any rice home from us. We were too hungry ourselves. I noticed Uncle Chen's shame on himself; and Mother and Father's guilt, because they could not help a friend.

But at least Uncle Chen could have gruel with us at lunchtime before leaving.

After that, I did not see him for a long time.

Chapter 23

I needed to talk to someone, to relieve my anxieties, so I went to Sun's home. But, there was sadness there too and the atmosphere was troubled. Jing just bowed her head down, focusing on sewing. Sun and her sisters said nothing.

No reading and hammering could be heard inside the house. I wondered if Ahn might be busy at the furnace site, or at school. I asked Sun in a low voice. She told me that once again, Ahn had been suspended without warning from his duties.

"He was denounced."

"What for?"

"For listening in the dark."

"Listening to what?"

"The enemy's radio."

"Enemy's... radio?"

"He just listened to the English program to improve his English."

"But he's good at English already."

"It's been his habit for many years."

"Did they send him to the Cadre School again?"

"This time he went to the Cowshed, a place for 'thought crime' people."

"Thought crime!"

"Yes."

"Have you told Moon?"

"She too has been purged ... in the army."

"What?"

"I can't explain it. We don't yet understand what is happening to her."

Sun told me that Jing had gone to the Cowshed to visit Ahn just a few days ago. Jing saw that he was suffering from hunger, but was still being forced to work hard. Sun described her father's appearance.

"Mother says he looks weak and has dropsy from hunger."

Her words reminded me of Uncle Chen. I pictured him as I'd last seen him, also weak and dropsical. Ahn is not the only one, I thought. This is happening everywhere. I banished the thought from my brain, because it scared me. We were silent for a moment, then, suddenly, Sun gave me a candy.

"Oh, my goodness! A candy! Where did you get it?"

Sun was silent for a while, then she told me that because Ahn was jailed in the Cowshed, their rations were reduced. Fortunately, her overseas relatives had mailed candy and biscuits to them, to help them survive.

"That bastard!"

"Who?"

"The postman."

"What did he do?"

Sun explained how Jing found the mail package always broken and its quantities did not match what the relatives had described in their letters. Jing suspected the postman had stolen their mailed food. But, she could do nothing about it.

"Mother took some to Father anyway," said Sun.

Soon after, I saw Ahn again at our school campus. But, he was not back to teach students. He was there as a political campaigns target for criticism by the general assembly. The school now scheduled these regularly and every time one was held, Ahn was brought in from the Cowshed for public criticism.

At the meetings, Ahn was usually silent, just standing on the stage of the school campus, watching the sky at first, until they forced him to bow his head to make him look shamed and guilty.

"You thought your daughter in army could protect you?"

"You thought you had powerful backing?"

"You're a spy!"

"Confess! How many orders have you accepted from the agent?"

"How dare you listen to enemy radio!"

At the Criticism by General Assembly, the crowds shouted at Ahn aloud, counting his crimes, questioning him, time and time again. I squeezed through the crowds to get closer to Ahn. He recognized me and murmured to the air.

"It was only my English language program..."

"You are a traitor!"

"Trying to cheat our Revolutionary Masses?"

"You are the only one who understands English -now you try to use it against your country!"

Ahn tried to defend himself at first, but it was useless. Nobody listened - they only shouted him down angrily. He fell to the floor and was dragged away. Then, another new political campaign target was brought onto the stage.

Sun and her family dared not go to the assembly, so after each meeting, I always ran to report to Sun.

"Why did he fall down? I asked her.

"He is hungry and exhausted. But Father does not mind being the political campaign's target."

"Why not?"

"Don't say this to anyone else, but he would rather be there than stay in the Cowshed."

Could this be true? I could not understand why anyone would choose to stand on the stage to endure so many cruel assaults.

My confusion lasted until the day I met Ahn at his home just after a meeting and sure enough, he seemed like a fresh man - tired but happy.

I asked him about it. Ahn was silent for a while, and then, he smiled shyly.

"It gives me a rest from the hard labor."

After this confession, Ahn seemed a little embarrassed and he even blushed. I gaped at him. Then, I went and told Sun what he'd said. She was silent and thoughtful at first but she suddenly sighed.

"There's more to it than that," she said. "They let him stay at home for one night, too."

Every time Ahn returned home to be the political campaign target for

Criticism by the General Assembly, he was allowed to have dinner with his family and stay over. But he had to leave next morning.

"To have him with us for that one night – it feels like a festival."

Now, I understood. It was worth it for Ahn to endure the stage because it meant he could relax at home afterwards. As I chatted softly with Sun, I could hear the familiar sounds of reading or hammering coming from inside Ahn's workshop. He seemed absorbed in his hobby.

It puzzled me. Was it just because summer was coming? Or was this something he missed deeply at the Cowshed?

Later, they gave Ahn a new mission. They forced him to clean the toilets. Sometimes I met him in the toilets in our town or at the school. At first, Ahn seemed embarrassed about it, but he quickly adapted to this new phase of his life.

He soon learned to ignore contemptuous glances from his old colleagues and students. He became happy and seemed more relaxed than before. Perhaps he was just pretending, but I was sure he smiled more after that.

I praised him while encountering him.

"You do a better job than the old janitor."

Ahn smiled at me.

"Would you like to learn English..."

His suggestion surprised me. I had not expected it. I hesitated to give him an answer at once, though he waited uneasily for my answer.

"I'll ask my parents..."

"It is up to you."

"How about Sun...?"

"She used to do it."

Suddenly Ahn spoke one sentence in English.

"I love Chairman Mao!"

Why did he say that so quickly? I had no time to respond. Ahn explained what it meant in both Chinese and English. Then I noticed something that helped me to understand.

My classmate Fatty had entered the toilet. Ahn stopped talking at once and went off with his bucket and broom. Fatty questioned me about the conversation he'd overheard.

"What were you talking about?"

"We were just chatting."

"Chatting? Using bird's language?"

"Yes!"

I left the toilet, but Fatty shouted after me.

"Who can believe that!"

At dinner time, I told my parents what had passed between Ahn and me, and asked Father's permission to learn English from Ahn.

Father said "NO," without hesitation, in his most serious voice.

My parents both seemed anxious about it.

"Why?" I asked them.

"Just look at Ahn's situation now. How has learning English helped him?"

"I've thrown everything out of my head that he taught me. He can keep it," said my brother.

"It's a useless language," said Mother, "and worse that, it gets people into trouble."

I had no reply, so I bowed my head and ate in silence.

Chapter 24

Later, I met Ahn again and told him that I was not allowed to learn English from him. But, Ahn seemed somehow absent. He just bowed his head and continued his work, as though he had not heard me.

Again, Fatty came in to spy on us. I glanced at him in disgust as he pissed aloud at the corner of the toilet. Then I calmed myself and walked outside, passing by the school office.

Many posters were pasted on the wall. The old posters were covered by new ones. Some of them were torn, waving in the wind. I found one there that was written by Father on my behalf.

At that time, pupils were too young to understand the Revolutionary Theory, so we were unable to write posters for ourselves, but we could sign ones that our parents had made for us.

In the past, the posters were hung on strings tied between trees. Now the trees were all cut down, the posters could only be stuck on school walls.

I walked along, browsing the wall.

Suddenly, one name erupted in my face. Moon. There it was on the poster. She was denounced for suicide! It was hard to believe what I was reading. She had killed herself for her crimes.

The poster explained that this put her father Ahn under suspicion too and deprived him of his powerful backing. It called for the Revolutionary Masses to dig out more about Ahn's crimes.

"Moon had committed suicide?"

I was stunned. Sun had given me no hint of any of this! Did she even know? What should I do? I had no idea. I hurried towards home. I encountered Sun herself in the pier as I passed the bridge. I spoke to her.

"What's happened?"

Sun said nothing at first, just sat at the edge of the pier, watching the stream in silence, her face clouded with sadness. Why did she choose this place to sit? Then I remembered summers of the past when all of us had swum here together, shouting and diving.

I remembered how the sisters had enjoyed watching the shining scales and vitality of the fish swimming in the river. I was never far away, usually chasing geese and ducks. Sometimes even Ahn sat fishing under the nearby willow tree, waving to us. Now everything had changed.

Suddenly, Sun interrupted my memories.

"Moon told us the truth in her letters..."

Then she explained that Moon had not died for the crime described in the denouncement poster, but for her beauty and her excellence on the stage. Then Sun told me everything she knew.

As a tailor's daughter, Moon loved beautiful clothes, and understood how to dress up to outshine all others, both on the stage, and in daily life. Men loved her. Women were jealous. Wherever she went, dangerous rumors shadowed her.

One evening, a senior officer watched her perform. To show his appreciation, he praised Moon, clapped his hands loudly and presented her with flowers. From the first time he saw her perform he pursued her. This kind of thing had happened to Moon before and she thought nothing of it at first; no-one could have foreseen how this story would end.

After that first night, the senior officer visited her regularly with invitations to dinners or parties. He also offered to introduce her into the officer training college.

However, Moon refused him, because she was in love with someone else - the leader of the troupe. But the senior officer did not give up. He invested more and more time and patience on his mission to win her heart. But nothing succeeded.

Soon the officer felt shamed by his failure. He grew jealous of the leader of the troupe. He began planning ugly ways to use the power of his senior rank to destroy his rival.

Moon knew the best way to stop the officer's pursuit was to marry her lover. But their marriage application was censored, and then rejected by the organization.

They were denied the right to marry, because of Moon's overseas background and because her father Ahn was a spy and rightist who had been detained at the Cadre School and the Cowshed.

The officer was so angry, he had the troupe leader jailed, thinking that without her lover's presence in her life, Moon would soon surrender. But, he was wrong. Moon still refused him. The officer could not control her, and in his fury he began treating her more harshly, and then he set her up for denouncement.

A slanderous rumor quickly spread, that she was a spy, a ticking bomb inside the army. After all, this woman could speak English. She could listen in to foreign language programs on the radio. It was easy to believe that she was receiving messages from enemy agents.

Moon was trialed in military court and sent to prison. Her long hair was cut off, and her head shaved bald. Her beautiful clothes were confiscated. Then they condemned her to hard work and semi-starvation in a forced-labor camp.

After a period of time, the officer suggested that if Moon would change her mind and surrender to him, he would remove her from the horrors of her cruel situation. But still Moon resisted him. The officer was now so angry he took steps to have the troupe leader purged. It was not long before Moon's lover was killed.

When she heard that her lover had died and her father Ahn had been sent to the Cowshed, Moon lost all hope and courage. She no longer wanted to live. She waited for the darkness of night and took the first chance to end her own life.

As Sun related her story, Moon's characters played in confusion across my brain, switching from spy to revolutionary and then to agent, as though in the model dramas we had once all practiced together. By the time Sun finished speaking, I was finding it difficult to breathe.

At that time I was too young to judge such complicated matters, so I clung to the simple facts I knew.

"Sun is a good girl; so was Moon ..."

I longed to comfort Sun, but I could find no words.

But still things got worse. Later that night, Ahn was again the political campaign target for Criticism by the General Assembly, but this time Fatty denounced Ahn for using the opportunity of his home stay-over's to draw pupils into his snares. He described Ahn trying to entice me in the toilet and Sun also enticing me with candy. It seemed he had been spying on me for some time.

According to Fatty, Ahn was secretly training spies, unaware that he was watched. Ahn was deprived of his last benefits and sent back to the Cowshed straight after the meeting. We cursed Fatty time and again, but were powerless to change the decision.

So Sun made a plan to get food to Ahn secretly. She was young enough that the militias did not pay her much attention. My own part was to distract the attention of the militias while Sun slipped close to Ahn and placed the food in his pocket.

I was a child and did not understand the risk I was taking. I only thought of it as a game - like something that might happen in a movie. Ahn knew what Sun had done but his face showed no change of expression. Then, the militias spotted us.

"Go away!" they shouted. "This is not a playground!"

Ahn walked on sadly without waving, because his hands were tied behind his back. He just turned his head just once, and looked our way as though he was trying to send us comfort, as he dragged himself away through the dust.

Sun waved to him, but Ahn could only respond with the expression in his eyes. We stayed watching until he disappeared in the distance. Only then did we turn our steps homeward.

When we were half way home, Sun stopped suddenly. She passed me a candy.

"You are brave!" she said.

Her voice was as sweet as the taste of the candy.

Chapter 25

One day, my brother told Father about his new plan to join the demonstration of Red Guards currently travelling the country. He said it was a great action to help China. Dad ordered my brother to shut up about it.

But my brother did not obey. He argued that all the best Red Guards in the country were involved in this campaign. They wanted only to carry the revolutionary experience nationwide.

"I can learn so much!"

"Don't you know, there is chaos everywhere?" said Father.

"The great leader Chairman Mao said that big chaos always accompanied big management."

"Bullshit!"

"How dare you say that!" my brother warned.

"Sit down! Eat your gruel!"

The argument raged, my brother passionate and aggressive and Father trying hard to control his anger. Mother did her best to placate them. The conflict was distressing to my sister and me. We were relieved when it was over at last.

My brother sat, eating quickly and swallowing loudly. Father withdrew inside himself and drank his gruel slowly. When I glanced at the faces of my parents, I noticed the worry in Mother's face and the signs of dropsy in both of them.

Father occasionally whispered to Mother.

"We are lucky."

"How?"

"We have rations."

It was an anxious lunch. Afterwards, my parents returned to work. Then my brother got busy packing. My sister and I followed him around inside the house, as he moved here and there, collecting what he needed.

"You're really going?"

"Yes!"

"But, you have no money."

"The tickets are provided for us."

"But, you have no food stamps," said my sister.

My brother paused to consider her words.

"That is a big problem."

He soon resumed packing, but his face was thoughtful. He went outside to discuss it with his classmates.

One afternoon, Mother sent me to take beans to my grandparents. She had been saving them up for a long time. I went out with the beans in a small paper bag, and walked as far as the bridge. Half way across, I encountered Fatty.

"Can you speak English now?" he jeered.

"Asshole, do you challenge me?"

Fatty laughed in my face. I retaliated.

"Motherfucker!"

The quarrel escalated to pushing and shoving. We were both too hungry to fight seriously, but the paper bag was torn and broken, and the beans rolled on the ground.

"Those are for my grandparents!"

"They have no teeth. How can they eat?"

Fatty grabbed some beans and ran away. I watched his back but lacked the energy, even to curse him. I straightened and breathed deeply. Then I knelt to pick up every bean, one by one, before continuing my journey.

When I arrived at my grandparents' home, I was surprised to see my brother there before me. He was explaining his travel plans to my grandparents.

He was begging them to help him realize his dream.

"I want to see Beijing city," he said.

"That's great!" said Grandma.

"I want to see our great leader, Chairman Mao!"

"That's wonderful too!"

"But I need your help. I have no food stamps."

"Have you discussed this with your parents? It is a chaotic world!"

Their lined faces showed the same signs of dropsy that I had noticed in my parents' faces.

Suddenly, grandpa slipped outside and asked my brother the same question again, quietly. My brother answered without turning his head.

"Yes!"

"What's their opinion?

"They're fine with it."

My grandparents thought it over, then gave him some food stamps, urging him to be careful. My brother departed with the food stamps.

That night, he asked me to keep this secret.

"Why should I keep quiet? I ought to tell Father."

He thought for a while, then, gave me two choices.

"A gift? Or a good beating? It's up to you. Which do you choose?"

"I want ... a gift."

"Smart choice!"

"But you have no money!"

"This is better than money. I'll write to you, telling you what I've seen."

I thought it over. I was so curious about those distant cities, especially our great capital Beijing. It was the heart of our country, the source of so much revolutionary news. I accepted the terms of the bargain.

My sister also wanted to join the great travelling demonstrations. But my brother persuaded her against it, for safety reasons.

"But what about your own safety?" she argued.

"You are a girl."

"Chairman Mao said that a woman can be half a sky!"

"Well, I'll go first while you stay home to help Mother. I'll share all my experiences with you, so you'll be better prepared when your own turn comes."

My sister accepted this. She asked my brother to write regularly, and give us every detail.

"No problem," he said.

He spent days preparing for his journey. He made lists of what he needed and of what he had already packed. He checked his lists and his pack
regularly as he gathered everything together. He did it all in secret,
keeping his backpack well hidden under the corner of his bed.

One morning, a few days later, after my Father and Mother had gone to
work, my brother brought his backpack out of hiding. He was excited
and nervous, checking it one more time. He put a five yuan note in his
wallet, and tied it up with a string.

"Where did you get the money!"

It was a big sum at that time. Was it from our grandparents? My brother
ignored my questions, and continued his preparations.

My sister put some papers and envelopes with stamps inside my brother's backpack. She checked and re-checked to make sure they were
okay. Only a girl would keep doing that, I thought.

"Keep your promise!" she urged.

"Take it easy."

"Have you got a pen?" she asked.

"It's already in my backpack."

My sister checked his backpack one last time to make sure that
everything was in place there. Then it was time to set out. My brother
went out to meet his team of fellow travelers.

My sister and I followed him through the streets until he found the
Red Guards on their way through. Their leader carried a big red flag;
it was waving in the wind. Others followed, full of excitement, bearing
backpacks or yellow canvas schoolbags.

They passed along the streets and then crossed the bridge, shouting

Revolutionary Slogans and singing the Red Revolutionary Songs. Once I saw them rest a while as though they were too hungry to shout and needed to save energy for their journey.

People crowded the streets as the marchers came to our primitive bus station. But they passed it by! Why? Were they so excited they'd forgotten to wait for the bus? Someone called to them.

"You're passing the bus station!"

"We walk to Beijing!"

"What!"

"It's a new Long March!"

"Ah!"

"Don't worry, we can do it."

My brother farewelled us and then ran to catch up with the marchers. I could see the red flag leading them on. We watched until it disappeared into the dust.

Even then, my sister and I stood there, waving at the fading dust cloud.

That evening, when Mother came home to prepare dinner, she asked us where our brother was. We evaded her question. Mother finished cooking, and took the dishes to the table.

"Go and find him," she said.

I pretended to look for him outside for a while, but of course I returned without him. Then Father became suspicious. He went to his bedroom. When he came out he looked angry and forced us to confess what we knew. He shouted at us with a grim face.

"Who stole my money? What's happened?"

I was fearful, but in the end I had to tell the truth. Dad found the bamboo stick, and gave both of us a good beating. Mother tried to stop him, but her efforts failed.

Because of his hunger, Father did not have the energy to beat us as long and hard as he once could. Mother tried to explain why he was so worried about my brother.

"You should not have helped him to go away," she said weakly. "There is too much danger and chaos in the world."

After dinner, Father and Mother rolled into bed earlier than usual, exhausted from hard work, probably wondering what other shocks the future might hold for them.

Days later, my brother kept his promise, and wrote his first letter to us. It was good news. He was alive and they had given up the walking, because of the tough road and the hunger. We all relaxed a little.

They were now traveling by train without tickets, as Red Guards were allowed to do, at that time. They were also specially privileged to take rest in school campuses and be served by campus staff. The Red Guards all shared their experiences with one another on the trains.

My brother told us that he had been to Beijing already. He had joined the crowds in the Tiananmen Square being reviewed by the great leader Chairman Mao.

"There were thousands and thousands of red flags everywhere, and thousands and thousands of Red Books in peoples' hands. It was a sea of red! The great leader Chairman Mao stood on the city gate tower of the Tiananmen Square, waving to us with his army cap! Wow! What a great moment! People were jumping and crying and shouting!"

Father read my brother's letter aloud. But, the excitement in the letter did not spread to me. Only my sister seemed to understand our brother's passion. I kept questioning while Father read the letter.

My sister jeered at me. "You don't understand because you are only a child!"

"When will he come back?"

"He does not say."

My brother emphasized one sentence near the end.

"We can eat as much as we like!"

This sentence affected us deeply. It made us so hungry. My mouth was watering while Father was reading.

Chapter 26

One day before lunch time, a stranger came to visit our house. He was a young man, about twenty years old. He wore dark clothes and his face was tanned. Even though he was noticeably dropsical from hunger, I could recognize that he had once been strong.

He seemed shy and a little embarrassed, as he stood at our gateway, introducing himself as Ge Ming, Uncle Chen's son. Father was surprised not to have recognized him at once.

"My God!" said Father, "You have grown up, and changed a lot!"

After his first surprise, Father was happy to see him but sorry for him too. He welcomed our guest warmly, inviting him into the house. Ge Ming stood in the center of the living room, holding a cloth bag in his hands. It seemed difficult for him to take the next step.

"Take a seat, please!"

"Well..."

An anxious expression crossed Father's face.

"How is your father?" he asked.

We had heard nothing of Uncle Chen for a long time. Mother entertained

Ge Ming with a cup of water. Ge Ming had to put down his bag on the ground.

Ge Ming sat nervously. He held the cup of water, but did not drink. His hands were trembling slightly. He seemed on the verge of tears, but he fought it and controlled himself.

"My dad has passed away."

"No!"

The news shocked us all. My wounded ankle throbbed again, as though to remind me of my old connection with Uncle Chen. Ge Ming told us that Uncle Chen died of hunger. I summoned up my last memory of Uncle Chen visiting us.

"He always said he was not hungry."

After calming himself, Ge Ming told us that his father always saved grains for his family. He described the famine existing in their village. It matched some of the rumors we'd heard about hunger around the country.

"People are so hungry they even ate their own dead."

We had heard rumors of this, but did not believe it. It was like a shadow in our minds, not something people would discuss openly. We tried to focus instead on the good news we saw in the newspapers. It seemed the people of our great country had so many achievements to celebrate.

Ge Ming resumed his sad story about his family, his father, and his villagers. My parents sympathized with him, listening carefully and sighing at the suffering he described.

After Ge Ming finished his story, Mother wanted to cook for him. But Ge Ming seemed suddenly to remember something and he tried to stop her.

He stood up, opening his bag quickly. There was white rice inside his bag! Where did he get from? He explained that he had come to thank us and repay some rice to us.

My parents protested. "There is no need to do this."

Ge Ming explained that his family had recently received a ration of rice from the grain storage of the People's Commune and his mother wanted to repay a share of it to us. Ge Ming used a bamboo bowl to scoop rice from his bag.

"My father said that you are the kind ones who helped us so much, and we should repay you several times over."

"That's silly! We had monthly rations."

Father grabbed Ge Ming's right hand firmly with his right hand, seizing the bowl with the other hand. The three adults argued and I could do nothing as their struggle continued.

"My Father gave me this mission as his dying wish!" said Ge Ming.

"We were old friends for many years and your father has also helped us a lot."

My parents tried hard to persuade him to keep his rice, but Ge Ming insisted on completing his father's mission. Perhaps my parents were too tired to continue the conflict, so in the end Ge Ming said good-bye and turned to go. Mother tried and failed to stop him leaving.

"You should have lunch before you go," she urged.

"Thank you but we have troubled you enough."

Father stood in the gateway, lost in thought, watching until Ge Ming disappeared at the corner of the street.

"God bless his family," Mother murmured.

Then she went to the kitchen to cook for us.

That seemed to be the end of it. Father returned to us in silence, staring at the floor. There were some rice grains scattered there and Mother collected each one carefully.

After lunch, I sat in the bamboo sofa, reading revolutionary comic books. It was boring and I felt sleepy. Suddenly, I heard shouting outside and the sounds of many people rushing by. I ran out to catch up with them.

"Hey, what's happening?"

"You don't know? They've opened the grain storage to the people!"

"Is that true?"

"Go! Go! Go!"

Many people were running to the grain storage and crowding around there with bags and baskets. They shouted and quarreled in the gateway of the building. But the militias used all their strength to push people back away from the fence.

"Go back!" they shouted.

But the people did not heed the warning of the guards and kept yelling and arguing with them. After a while, the crowds pushed so hard, the fence of the grain storage collapsed and the guards were forced back against the wall of the grain storage. This was an emergency.

The leader of the guards seemed to panic.

"Stop!"he shouted, "Or I'll shoot!"

His shouts failed to deter the stream of people flooding closer. He fired a warning shot into the sky.

It shocked the people to silence and halted their onrush.

"The grain store is only open to farmers. You must register first, one by one, with certificate!"

"The farmers are not the only ones who are hungry. We are also suffering!"

"Town residents have been rationed monthly!"

"But it's not enough for us."

"You're better off than the farmers!"

By now, the leader of the guards was using a loud-speaker. The militias brandished their guns to force people back outside the fence-line.

But the farmers could wait no longer. They rushed shouting into the entrance to get at their rations. The town residents crowded the gateway behind them, shouting and swearing.

I squeezed out of that crowd of people, where some were disappointed and others happy. I guessed that Ge Ming had gone there before visiting us. He must have got through before the news had spread throughout the town.

When my parents heard the news, their anxiety for Uncle Chen's family and the farmers eased a little.

My mom prayed for them.

"Perhaps they can breathe again now..."

It gave us hope that all of us might overcome this tough time. Suddenly, my sister recited a quotation of our great leader Chairman Mao to us.

"Hold on to the fight to victory!"

Later, Ge Ming visited again. This time, he brought rice pastry as a gift. He did not say too much, just explaining that he had dealings in town and came to visit on his way.

"Mother cooked it for you," he said.

"How is your mother?"

"She is fine."

"You should stay for lunch."

"Thank you for offering."

He put down the gift and walked away quickly.

That evening, Mother fried the rice pastry and shared it out between us. It was soft and wonderful to taste. Father gave his share to me. Mother gave him a dish with some fried beans in it.

Father ate no rice, just beans and alcohol. Where did he get enough energy for himself? He sipped, and then put one bean in his mouth, which he chewed for a long time.

I was curious, but he seemed to enjoy the moment so I did not ask and he did not explain. Only occasionally throughout that meal, did his face revert to its usual anxious expression.

Suddenly, my sister asked Father a question.

"When will my brother come home?"

"Soon," he reassured her.

Chapter 27

My brother came home at the beginning of summer, arriving at 8 pm, after our dinner time. He seemed tired from his long journey, but excited. After unloading his backpack, he spoke little but went straight to bed and slept all that night and the following day. Mom woke him for dinner next day. Even then, he still seemed sleepy.

"Wash your hands and face..."

My brother hesitated before obeying her, as though he was too sleepy to respond. We began the meal. My sister and I wanted to hear my brother's story from his own mouth.

My brother said nothing at first, just ate and swallowed quickly. Suddenly, he stopped eating and took a deep breath.

"We ate steamed breads every day!"

Then he became strangely talkative for the rest of dinner time, chattering with lively gestures, as though he was drunk.

My sister and I stopped eating and stared at him wide-eyed, following him with our imaginations as he described his travels over the mountains and into the outside world of big events and campaigns.

My brother and other Red Guards had marched miles and miles he said, then ridden in cars or trains, crossing hundreds and thousands of mountains and rivers and cities and lakes, arriving at last at Beijing, the great national capital of China.

"It was like a sea of red!"

"We saw him far in the distance..."

"Who?"

"Our great leader, Chairman Mao! He was waving his army cap from the city gate tower of the Tiananmen Square."

"He is our great leader!"

"Yes, he was waving to me! The crowds were going crazy!"

"Everyone was so excited, people could not control themselves and they waved their Red Books, jumping and shouting Revolutionary Slogans, singing Red Revolutionary Songs, tears in all of our faces. Live forever great leader Chairman Mao! It was the great happy moment for everyone!"

My brother, hardly able to control his own emotions began to sing the famous song The East Is Red in a low voice.

"The east is red, the sun rises..."

He seemed lost in his memories of the great moment. My sister and I admired him so much. My sister asked many questions.

"What other fun did you have?"

My brother stopped talking, thinking for a while, but suddenly he laughed aloud.

"We could find no place to piss in the Tiananmen Square."

We saw the humor in that, so we laughed too, except Father who stayed strangely serious.

Father did not interrupt. He just kept drinking while my brother talked on. At one point he seemed about to laugh, but he quickly controlled himself.

"Yes, it was a big problem there."

"How did you all deal with it?"

"We stood to form a defensive human screen around the pissing one..."

"My goodness!"

My brother stood, choking with laughter, and demonstrated the postures they had taken to create the screen.

"You had no option at the time."

"There were thousands and thousands of people around us. Have you ever heard someone say 'a people moutain' or 'a sea of people?' Well there you could truly understand what that means."

"Was it like our school campus?"

"Don't make me laugh. It's no comparison. You have no idea what a spectacle it was. Thousands and thousands of people crowded into one huge square. You could not get away from people. Everyone sweating and breathing the same air. Everyone hoarse from shouting. I lost my voice for days."

My sister wanted more funny stories. My brother thought for a moment, then quietly asked us if we could keep a secret. Of course, my sister and I both promised.

"After the crowds dispersed, someone picked up gold bars that had been left behind on the ground. "

"Wow!"

He explained that the Red Guards might have raided someone's home; then gone to the square for the review, before they had time to hide the gold. Or perhaps they just did not care about it that much. The bars might have dropped from their pockets while they were cheering and jumping for Chairman Mao.

"Did you find one yourself?"

"No."

"Is that true?"

"We only heard the rumor. We did not see the gold."

"Ah! But still it could be true."

We regretted he had found no gold himself, but he seemed not to care too much. Then he remembered another story, about a man who must be one of the happiest people in the world. By his tone, we knew that he admired the guy very much.

"Why is he so happy?"

"He was elected to be a representative of the Red Guards in the square to shake hands with the great leader Chairman Mao!"

"Shake hands with Chairman Mao! What a privilege!"

"He did not wash his hands anymore after the meeting!"

"Why not?"

"His hands had touched with Mao's."

"Ah!"

"What happened to him afterwards?"

"He had a new job after that. Just shaking hands with people every day. Everyone wanted to because they thought it was the same as shaking hands with Chairman Mao!

He was happy to pass on his experience and happiness to others in that way. He became a legend because of Chairman Mao. He kept telling people that Mao was so tall and his palm was so big and warm."

I tried to imagine how it would feel. I raised my head and glanced at the portrait of Chairman Mao on the wall. The smile from the portrait was mysterious and authoritative but wordless as always.

Beneath the portrait were several red books containing the collected quotations of Chairman Mao. They were known to us simply as Red Books.

I did not understand the quotations, but, I could repeat them fluently, because my parents were required to read them every day. It sounded a little like monks chanting.

Later, my brother also showed us the new Loyalty Dance for Chairman Mao. First he went to the desk and took a Red Book in his hand. Then he moved into the center of the house, dancing and waving the Red Book as he shouted passionate quotes from Chairman Mao, to coordinate with his dance steps. Never before had I seen any dance so wild, weird, and exaggerated.

"We practiced it all time."

"It's just crazy."

"What did you say?" said my brother in a warning tone.

Father interrupted suddenly.

"It's time to sleep."

Father had finished his dinner by this time. My sister was still absorbed by my brother's stories. She argued that it was too early to sleep yet. But, Mother began clearing the table.

"Your brother is tired. I need you to help me now."

"I am not tired, I've slept enough already."

"Your father and I have to get up early tomorrow."

My brother seemed disappointed and unwilling to go to bed, because he had so much more to tell. But he was soon asleep and snoring loudly like Father.

Father himself did not snore that night. I wondered if he'd gone to bed too early to sleep, or perhaps my brother's stories had interested him more than he showed, and he was lying awake, thinking them over.

I passed on my brother's stories to Sun. She seemed uninterested and passed no opinion when I finished. It was a long time since she'd talked much to me. I guessed that her experiences were changing her.

Her family situation had grown too weak. Ahn was in prison in the Cowshed; Moon had died; Jing had been forced to physical labor in the furnace site. Everyone jeered at Sun and her family these days.

"You can't just do what you like!" they shouted.

"You are the child of a capitalist!"

"What the hell are those colorful clothes you're wearing? Those are not for proletarians! Only capitalists wear them."

And as usual, Fatty was the one who used the most degrading language.

Chapter 28

After my brother and his classmates returned from Beijing, things changed a lot. They had learnt many new ways to torture the political campaign targets under Criticism by the General Assembly. The new methods scared people, but there were some crazy ones who enjoyed watching it.

One afternoon, I was fishing in the river bank. Someone passed by and shouted to me.

"Let's go!"

"What's happening?"

"Big deal!"

I hesitated, then made the decision-to follow them with my fishing rod, to the school campus. Most of us had learned by now to follow the mainstream into activities.

Thousands of people were already gathering in the school campus. Red flags were waving in the wind. The air was full of Revolutionary Songs being broadcast through the loud-speakers. People chatted and carried colorful placards.

The assembly host tapped the microphone with his finger to test if it was okay, and then, he shouted.

"Attention, now! Silence please!"

The crowds obeyed.

First the assembly host updated us on the new situation of the country and the latest guides from Chairman Mao. Then the political campaigns targets were taken up to the stage for criticism.

Ahn was among them as usual. He had a strange new hair-cut. Half of his head had been shaved so he was one half bald. A big placard holding his name and accusation, hung around his neck in front of his chest. Two militias kept his hands trapped behind him.

The host shouted at Ahn.

"Kneel down!"

But Ahn refused to kneel. So the militias kicked out his legs, forcing him to his knees. Ahn struggled fruitlessly. The militias held him down securely.

The host announced that Ahn had failed to confess his crimes and had tried to bribe someone to become a spy, using biscuits and candy that his overseas relatives had mailed to him.

"How can that be true? He almost starved to death!" someone called.

"You dare to slander our great socialism? There is no hunger in this great country!"

Not only did Ahn refuse to confess his crimes, but he also tried to defend himself. That made the host so angry, he stood up from his chair, pointing at Ahn with his finger and shouting through the loud-speakers at him. The crowds imitated his shouts, raising their fists to show their fury.

The shouting echoed into the distance.

Then the host announced that the Red Guards had brought new skills from the great capital Beijing, to fight the enemy. Several Red Guards went up to the stage, carrying top hats made of bamboo sticks and white paper.

Everyone wondered what would happen next.

"What new skills?"

"What will they do?"

People watched wide-eyed as the Red Guards surrounded Ahn, shouting accusations and slapping his face from one side to the other. They smeared graffiti onto Ahn's face with ink.

As I listened to the sounds of the slapping, my heartbeat accelerated. I feared to see what might happen next. But yet, I had to know, so I squeezed close to the front of the stage.

My brother went up to slap Ahn and I shouted to him aloud.

"Brother, you can't do that!"

My voice was lost in the noise of the crowd. But because I was so close to the edge of the stage, I was sure that my brother had heard or seen me.

He hesitated, but still he slapped Ahn on his face, but not with his full strength. I knew only too well how hard my brother could slap.

Suddenly, Fatty rushed onto the stage, denouncing Ahn for bribing children with gifts of candy or biscuits. He saw me in the crowd and pointed at me, shouting angrily.

"He's an example!"

Fatty rushed to the edge of the stage and jumped down in front of me. He grabbed my fishing rod and carried it onto the stage. He spoke to the other Red Guards. Then, Fatty announced he would demonstrate a new skill for fighting the enemy.

The Red Guards disappeared from the stage and people waited until they returned, all now carrying fishing rods. No-one could have guessed what they would do with them.

The Red Guards surrounded Ahn at a distance, cast the fishhooks towards him, and jerked them back, as though they were fishing in the river. But this was no fish, this was human prey!

The sharp hooks caught in Ahn's flesh of his ears, his nose, his face, his body. He cried aloud with the pain. Fatty and the Red Guards were laughing, shouting and cursing at him.

"See, this big fish!"

"We've caught a big fish hiding in deep water."

"Spy!"

"This is our retribution!"

The crowd was shocked by the cruelty at first, but soon they were swept up into it. They too shouted at Ahn. In minutes, Ahn's face and ears and nose and body were covered with blood and hooks. His clothes were torn and covered with blood. He shook all over, but the abuse continued.

Suddenly, someone shouted.

"Put his wife up there beside him!"

Others responded. Soon after, Jing was taken onto the stage. Fatty's father Lee rushed at her, pointing angrily, and denouncing her as the saboteur who had destroyed his overalls.

I suddenly remembered the day that Lee had argued with Jing over her sewing fees. He had warned her then that one day she would pay for it. Now it seemed that day had come.

Lee grabbed Jing's hair and slapped her face from side to side. The crowds responded with crazed shouting. Jing staggered under the attack. Lee kept kicking her, spitting and cursing. He shouted at her again and again.

"You think your clothes more beautiful than ours?"

"You think our clothes are ugly?"

"You're a beauty snake!"

"You're a colour demon!"

Fatty also came up to slap Jing's face and he abused her with an old remembered jealousy.

"She bribes children with fig syrup!"

There was nothing Jing could say or do to help herself. No one would listen to her self-defense and no one would believe her. She was slapped and shoved, here and there, until she fell at last with blood seeping from her lips

Ahn struggled to try and reach her. But the Red Guards prevented him. He could do nothing but shed helpless tears.

After that, both Ahn and Jing were forced to wear top hats. The hats were as tall as my fishing rod. The two of them were taken from the stage, and publicly exhibited in the town center, wearing those ugly hats.

They were paraded as enemies in the main street, leashed with ropes by the Red Guards. Their top hats shook as they walked slowly among crowds who cursed them.

I ran from the scene and on to Sun's home. I arrived to find Sun squatting terrified in a corner, unresponsive to anything. Her sister Star was trying but failing to comfort her.

Sun's arms were wrapped around her knees and her eyes stared into space. I could not talk to her like that, so I just stayed quietly beside her for a while and then went home.

At dinner, Father was silent at first, but as he sat drinking his anxiety became more obvious. He began to talk. Then stopped, dissatisfied about something. He criticized my brother for dropping rice on the table.

"Pick up that rice!" he growled.

"Why? It's nothing."

"Put it in your bowl!"

"What is wrong with you?" said my brother.

Father made a big deal of the rice, though it was nothing to my brother. After a short argument, Father sat for a while brooding silently and drinking his rice wine. Then he went slowly to the door, found the bamboo stick, walked back to my brother and gave him a good beating.

My brother stood up and tried to avoid the attack.

But Father continued beating him and shouting in fury.

"You think you have learnt something worth bringing back?"

At that moment, my brother was really afraid, trying and failing to protect himself with his hands. He ran to Mother.

Mother tried to protect him but she could not. In the end my brother had to run from the house to escape. We did not fully understand Father's fury. After my brother ran away, father sat down again, drinking and cursing.

"Crazy creature!" he muttered.

Mother was anxious about Father's words and tried to stop him saying more. "Not so loud!" she said, "Someone might hear!"

Later, I guessed that Father was angry because my brother had slapped Ahn. But my parents must keep themselves out of trouble.

"Just be good to everyone!" they warned us.

Chapter 29

One hot summer day, I invited Sun to go swimming in the river with me. But she was not interested. Disappointed, I went to the river alone.

The appetites of the furnaces had ensured there were no longer any trees in sight there. All had been cut down to feed their big bellies. Now there was no escape from the heat and dazzle of the sun.

I sweated and wanted to strip off my sweaty garments, but to avoid the worse pain of sunburn, I kept them on and bore the discomfort.

At the river bank, I looked for dog's tail grass. I picked one, cleaned the tip and wrapped spider webs around it to form a ball. I shook it in front of a dragonfly.

The dragonfly thought the web-ball was food. Was it blind? It flew onto it, but stuck to the sticky ball and was trapped. The dragonfly struggled with his all strength, but could not escape the spider-web ball.

Another of my games was to catch dragonflies by their wings, play with them for a while, then let them fly away. When I was alone, such games killed time. I liked the cicadas too, but, they had gone.

A dragonfly has sharp teeth in his mouth.

It was too hot to stay in the sun. I took off my clothes, jumped into the water and dived deep. Wow! So cool and soothing. There were hardly any fish in the river. Hungry townspeople had caught most of them by that time.

I remembered using dragonflies or earthworms as bait and suddenly I wanted to do it again. But my fishing rod had been taken by Fatty at the assembly so it was impossible now.

"Son of a bitch!"

I shouted as I swam. I glanced towards the pier. No one was there. In all that dazzling sunshine, how I missed the shade of the old willow tree, the sight of Ahn beneath it and even the fish themselves which had been so plentiful then.

I swam to the bridge, and hid in its cool shadows. After a while, I heard the sound of people hurrying across above my head. I swam out to see what was going on.

Fatty was there and he leaned against the fence of the bridge.

"Hey! Come with me," he shouted.

"Go to a hell!" I replied.

"What's wrong with you?"

"You're a bastard!"

He just smiled, "We go to confiscate Sun's house!"

"You asshole!" I said.

Then he gave me a proud salute and ran away.

After Fatty had gone, I swam around for a bit longer. But I needed to know what was happening at Sun's house, so I climbed out, dressed quickly and ran.

Before I even got to the corner nearest to Sun's home, I met excited people, happily carrying away furniture or clothes.

After turning the corner, I saw people crowded in front of Sun's gate-way. A figure slipped out of the crowds and ran away quickly? Was it my brother? At this distance I could not be sure.

The people were shouting and cursing at the family, who stood by watching helplessly. Jing was sobbing, holding Sun to her chest. Sun did not cry, just shut her lips tightly, watching in silence.

Fatty was coming in and out bringing things from the house. He threw comic books on the ground. Fatty's father Lee threw colorful clothes over the books, then lit it with a match. The flames rose and consumed it all - books, clothes and other things that Sun's family had owned.

Lee shouted to Jing.

"You must move out before tomorrow! How dare you live in a villa!"

Everyone left carrying something that had belonged to the family. Fatty walked out of the house with a box I recognized as Ahn's. There were fishing lines and hooks inside it.

"If you want some, you'll have to beg," said Fatty as he carried it by me.

I glared at him. The father and son walked away proudly. I spat at their retreating backs, then went to Sun. Jing spoke to me with a lifeless voice.

"Baoguo, this is not your business. Go home!"

Later, at home, I caught my brother sneaking in. I asked him why he was so stealthy. He did not answer me at first, just put a finger to his lips, signaling me to silence.

But I was angry, and raised my voice.

"You!"

He took a comic book from his pocket and showed it to me.

"Okay, I was there but I did no bad thing. Look, I stole this for you, before it was burnt like all the others."

"You bastard!"

"And I did not hurt Ahn very much that day on the stage. Others attacked him heavily. I was secretly trying to protect him from them."

I did not believe him. He sighed deeply.

"Keep this to yourself," he said, holding out the comic book.

I replied only with silence.

"Keep it in a secret place."

"I'll tell our parents!"

"I'll give you a good beating if you do."

He put the comic book into my palm and slipped outside again quietly. I browsed through it and saw bloodstains on the pages. I tried and failed to clean them off.

I wrapped the book with paper, and hid it in my school bag. Then I sat in the bamboo sofa, staring at the schoolbag and wondering if it was a safe enough place. Soon I took the comic book out and hid it somewhere else. I tried hiding place after hiding place, but nowhere felt safe enough.

Eventually I went to sleep on the bamboo sofa. My sleep was short. I woke in a sweat from some horrible dreams.

Once my parents were home, my brother kept glancing my way every moment. I knew what was worrying him. But I had no great urge to relate the events of that day to Mother and Father.

Mother glanced my way and spoke.

"I heard Sun's family have to find somewhere else to live."

I pretended not to know. So did my brother.

"Oh? Well, I can soon ask her to see if it's true. I played with my brother today."

Dad looked at my brother, then at me. At first he tried to signal me with his eyes. I murmured some half-response. Suddenly, my dad lost interest in trying to dig something out of us.

Mother turned to my sister.

"What did you do today?"

"I went to help Grandma and Grandpa."

"Good girl. Remember, you're a girl."

"We can be half a sky."

Mother worried about my sister, but did not want to argue with her.

I could not sleep that night and lay tossing and sweating in my bed, reliving the horrors of the day while the mosquitoes whined outside my net.

Around midnight I began to doze, but was suddenly woken by noise outside. At first, I thought it was another nightmare. Then I heard the urgent voice of the announcer of the People's Commune, demanding attention through the loud-speakers. His voice was so loud and compelling, it woke every resident of the town, urging the people to assemble.

Why? To listen to the latest achievements and guides from Chairman Mao.

My parents woke, dressed in a panic, and rushed to the assembly. They sat listening to the reports, and afterwards they participated in the organized celebratory parade in the town center.

I could hear drums and gongs and people running through the streets, shouting the Revolutionary Slogans and singing the Red Revolutionary Songs for the latest victories. It was a sleepless night for the whole town.

Chapter 30

One afternoon, I sat in the heat, longing to go fishing. I could make a fishing rod easily enough with bamboo but no one in our town could make good fishhooks, except Ahn.

As I knew, Fatty had taken away all Ahn's hooks and lines, even the gear and tools. I remembered him asking me to beg for them, but I would never beg anything from that bastard.

I could do nothing but think and dream. I lay on the bamboo sofa, imagining I was strong enough to give Fatty a good beating. Many such thoughts swirled through my brain before I dozed off at last.

Suddenly, I was woken by shouting and singing outside. What was happening this time? I slipped outside and walked towards the town center.

It was hot. The cicadas which had sung every summer of my life were silent now. I remembered climbing trees to catch cicadas and pressing their backs to make them sing. It was one of my favorite games, but that was in the past now, like fishing.

Summer seemed strange without the music of birds and cicadas. The only songs we heard now were "Red" and "Revolutionary".

I stood on the bridge and stared into the distance. Smoke rose from the furnace chimneys and filled the sky with gloom.

Then I saw Sun coming towards me. I asked her where she was going.

"To buy soy sauce," she said, without raising her head.

I followed her, chatting away. She listened but did not reply.

She entered the grocery store and put the bottle on the counter. The clerk put a funnel into the mouth of the bottle, then scooped soy sauce from the jar on the ground, through the funnel into the bottle. Sun gave him money and ration stamps.

Sun left the grocery store and turned for home in a hurry. Again, I followed, and it seemed to make her a little anxious and angry. She tried to stop me, but I would not turn back. I had not visited her new home yet.

It was a long walk and the house was very different from the one she had lived in before, just a small flat in a suburb of the town. It had a tile roof, mud brick walls, beaten earth floor, and small windows. The sewing machines were close to a window.

I could not help comparing it to where she had lived before. Previously, her family was the only one in our town to live in a two-story building made of concrete and bricks - a wonderful place full of fairy tales and colorful clothes and song and laughter.

"You must understand our situation has changed," she said.

Jing was surprised to see me. She smiled at me but kept busy at her work in the tiny room. She had to bow her head down, close to the machine, because in the dark room it was so hard to see the details. I was surprised they had let her keep the sewing machine.

"They still need my sewing skills," she explained.

I had not seen Sun in school for some days, since someone had angered her by calling her a "pup of the spy." She could not defend herself, for fear of retaliation from Fatty and his followers, so she was afraid to go to school.

"How are you?" I asked.

"You're here now. You can see how we must live."

I could think of no reply.

"But at least it's quiet here. It's easier to avoid notice. And it may be small, but we can keep it tidy."

Then Sun and I began to talk. We spoke in low voices, but we opened our minds to each other and it made us happy. It was our first good talk in a long time and it helped me to understand what her family was going through at the time.

When we stopped talking at last, the only sound inside the house was the whirring of the sewing machine.

Suddenly, the silence was broken. People rushed into the house without warning. They were all wearing red armbands and they crowded in shouting. They began searching and checking everywhere. There were so many people in that small house, it was hard for me to breathe.

Lee was among them. He yelled at me.

"What are you doing here?"

"Nothing."

"Be careful! They'll bribe you."

I made no reply.

Jing spoke in a low voice.

"Why are you here? What more can you take from us?"

"We have not finished with you yet," said Lee. "You should know we may come at any moment to make sure you are not hiding anything."

Then he stood in the center of the house and looked around.

"This place is suitable for you!" he said to Jing.

His people checked every corner of the house, but found nothing suspect. It was like a game to them and they seemed disappointed when it had such a flat ending. Before leaving, Lee ordered Jing to accompany Ahn at the next assembly.

"It's this afternoon," he said. "You are a spy like him, so you must be there too. You are both monsters!"

Jing listened to their abuse in silence. I could not understand how a bastard like Lee could so easily change his fortunes from victim to oppressor.

My dad had told us that Lee had learnt lessons from the Revolutionary Movements, and become a pioneer in the follow-up campaigns. He was useful to the leader of his unit, because of his cruelty and cunning.

Lee soon became a leader of the rebels. He learned to spy on the "Five Types of People" who were the enemy of the proletariat, and next he began working as a host and activist in the Criticisms by General Assembly.

His other great advantage was being the master chef in our town. Leaders entertaining high-ranked officers from the big cities, could not do without Lee. He could satisfy all of them. He worked hard, and grabbed every chance that came his way. It was an open secret.

The first time he took his position as host of a meeting, he panicked and used the wrong words, making a fool of himself.

"Comrades," he said, "Be quiet! It is dinner time!"

People gaped and laughed aloud at what he had said.

However, since then he had gained experience and become an efficient host of the assembly.

Jealous people ridiculed him, but always privately.

"Dead fish revived!" they said.

They dared not complain about him in public, because he was no longer the person he had once been.

After Jing moved out of the house she had lived in, Lee moved into it. Many envied him, but could do nothing, because Lee was so powerful now.

That afternoon, I followed along to the school campus. The loud-speakers were broadcasting Red Revolutionary Songs. People crowded around the stage. Lee sat at the desk, and his harsh voice announced the start of the meeting.

"Attention! Silence please!"

Ahn's name was called and he was taken onto the stage. He looked weak, hardly able to stand on his own feet. He endured the militias' treatment without struggling as once again they hurried to shave his hair.

As before, they shaved only half of his head. Half bald, he looked like a ghost. It was the hairstyle known as *yin yang tou* in China.

A Red Guard slapped his face, and forced him to bow his head down.

After a while, Jing was taken up to the stage to suffer abuses alongside her husband. Fatty went to her with scissors. First he cut her hair in the same ugly style. Then he cut holes in her clothes.

Red Guards smeared ink on the faces of Ahn and Jing. The audience catcalled and laughed. Then, Lee called the militias to take a bucket up to the stage.

"What's in the bucket?"

"This is a secret weapon."

"What's that smell?"

Lee ordered Ahn and Jing to kneel. Then, he poured the contents of the bucket over their heads.

What the hell! It was urine!

Those militias stepped back to avoid contamination. The stench assaulted everyone there.

People shouted and held their noses. Some felt sick and nauseous. Others protested in low voices. Ahn and Jing both collapsed to the ground. Then they were dragged off to be paraded in the main street.

On their way to the town center, the militias tried to avoid touching the bodies of Ahn and Jing. Their disgust at the smell made them keep their distance from the couple. It gave Ahn his one opportunity.

Passing over the bridge, Ahn took his chance to jump into the river. He struggled in the water for a few seconds, then disappeared under the surface. Everyone stood motionless as though stunned.

Meanwhile the current in the river carried Ahn quickly downstream, far away from us all. In just one moment, he had escaped successfully, from hell on earth to heaven in the water.

The militias soon came to their senses but were slow to take any action. Jing screamed and then collapsed near the railing of the bridge. At the same moment, several militias began running downstream to begin searching.

But, it was all too late.

With his hands tied behind him, Ahn was unable to keep himself afloat and he swallowed water and drowned quickly. The river carried him so far, it took them a long time to find his body.

As I watched them bring him ashore at last, my body began to shake. I felt chilled despite the strong sunshine. All I could hear was the sound of my own teeth chattering. Many people around me became hysterical.

Mother rushed to Jing. She ignored the smell, squatted down and held her head, pressing her thumb onto Jing's face in the spot called *Ren Zhong* zone between her nose and lips, trying to help her in the traditional Chinese way.

Lee stood murmuring and cursing over and over, as though he had no idea what to do next. Then, he went to check Ahn's body. He pressed one side of Ahn's neck, his face skeptical.

"Are you really dead?"

He reached out his finger to check Ahn's nostrils. But- Ahn could no longer hear nor answer any question Lee might ask him. Ahn's belly was a horrible sight, distended like the belly of a pregnant woman. I wanted to walk away, but could not move my feet.

Lee shouted aloud at Ahn's body.

"He is an outlaw!"

"Committed suicide!"

"This outlaw used to catch fish. He's a dead fish now!"

Chapter 31

Seven days after Ahn's death, his family held a memorial ceremony for him. Jing and her daughters came to the bridge and placed a cup on the spot where Ahn had jumped. They filled it with alcohol, lit incense, and threw dumplings into the river.

Then, Jing led the family members in kneeling, kowtowing downstream over the river, in the customary homage that families pay to their dead.

People began to gather on both sides of the bridge, all watching the family's actions. Soon, the crowd was big enough to block the bridge.

Jing's family all wore white sackcloth, and their faces were serious and sad. Never before had I seen them so solemn, so silent. That was the first time they had appeared together in public since Ahn's death. I heard low-voiced sympathy coming from the crowd.

"What a pity!"

"They are beautiful girls."

Suddenly, I saw Fatty slipping quietly away from the crowd. No one noticed him but me. Somehow I guessed that whatever he was up to, it was nothing good.

A little later, I heard shouting just beyond the crowd, and more chaotic noise as someone forced their way through. Then Fatty's father Lee, accompanied by several militias lunged through into the center of the crowd.

"Get out of here! Stop these superstitious activities! Are you trying to call up his evil spirit?"

First Lee banished the audience.

"Everyone, get back to work at the furnace site!"

Next he shouted at the family, broke the alcohol bottle and cup, smashed the incense, and kicked at Jing. He drove the family off the bridge.

Seeing things like this always frightened me. But something always drove me to be there, to see every little thing that happened. I had to know.

From then on, Jing had to spend more time in the furnace site. She labored hard, and always Lee dogged her steps, flaunting his red armband, monitoring her, shouting at her with ceaseless aggression.

"I'm watching you! Work harder! This is no time to be lazy!"

She was his constant scapegoat and he made her a public example, hoping everyone would see and hear his treatment of her. He seemed to enjoy the feeling that he was demonstrating the dictatorship of the proletariat.

At first, Sun and her sisters were also expected to work with their mother, but Star made a mistake that almost destroyed one of the furnaces. It angered the leader of the furnace site. They accused Star of sabotage. They beat her and locked her up for weeks.

After that, Jing's daughters were not allowed to labor in the furnace site, for fear of further sabotage. But I went there myself so that I could keep Sun informed about everything that was happening. She did not expect me to do this, but I knew she was keen to know that Jing was okay.

At the furnace site, Jing had to lift heavy loads; broken chunks of steel and iron, firewood, coal, etc. They forced her to transport them at speed under the blazing sun.

Sweat soaked her clothes and glued her hair to her dirty face and forehead. Her body and clothes were caked with dirt, her beautiful white fingers scratched, the nails broken. She wore a straw hat all the time, to cover her ugly *yin yang tou*.

When the militias caught me hanging about near the furnace they drove me away, sometimes forcing me to run here and there until the heat exhausted me. When it got too hot to bear, I could run away and find somewhere to hide from the strong sunshine, but, Jing had no such escape. She must stay and continue her work.

I went to the river and jumped into the water. I swam and dived for a while, then rested under the bridge. It was cooler there in the shade, and the water was quiet.

I turned to look downstream and thought about fishing, but fishing reminded me of Ahn and the memories clung. Suddenly, I sensed some weird presence surrounding me, coming from under the water, as though something was watching me from deep below.

Was there something there? I scrambled out into the heat of the sun and quickly dressed myself. My body was soon hot but my spirit was chilled. I took one more frightened look downstream, then ran for home as fast as I could, to get away from that place.

My brother was surprised to see me arrive.

"Hey! What's happening?"

"I'm cold."

"How can you be cold?"

"Then maybe I'm scared."

"Scared of what?"

"Maybe Ahn..."

"He's dead!"

"That's what scares me."

I took a deep breath, and poured water to drink. After that, I calmed down and slipped outside again. I went to Sun's home to talk to her.

Sun sat watching Star sewing. Star often assisted with her mother's work. Meanwhile, I related everything happening at the furnace site to Sun. She said little, but thanked me with her eyes.

When Jing came home, she flung off her dirty work clothes, took a long shower, then dressed in clean clothes. Now she was fresh and tidy again.

To hide her shameful hair style, she wrapped a bright scarf around her head. Oh, how it suited her! The special pretty woman we knew had returned.

But her neck was browner than before and she could not hide the abrasions on her fingers and palms. Sun took a tape from a drawer, and dressed her mother's wounded hands.

Then, Jing replaced Star at the sewing machine. She bowed her head to the task, enjoying her task of fixing the pieces of cloth together into clothes. Suddenly, she seemed to remember me, still in the house.

"Hey, you should go home."

I hesitated, unwilling to leave, but, thinking they might have things to discuss privately, I said goodbye to Sun. She thanked me.

Just as I was leaving Jing smiled at me, speaking in a strange language. I did not understand what she said, but I saw gratitude in her eyes.

Later, Sun translated her mother's English sentence into Chinese for me.

"She thanks you very much!"

It made me thoughtful.

Chapter 32

At dinner time, my parents discussed the furnaces.

"They're saying the products are not up to professional standard," said Father. "We're failing because we have not enough expertise, so all that we invested was a waste. That furnace is nothing but a big lump of iron."

My brother chipped in.

"Can China still catch up to the British and US imperialism in our plan?"

"Children should not interrupt adults talking," said Father.

"But I'm a Red Guard!"

In our house, my brother was rarely accorded the respect he thought he deserved. My father ignored his Red Guard status and treated him no differently from his other children. The two of them often clashed. I just kept eating and listening.

Next day, another Criticism by General Assembly was held in the furnace site. It was Lee's idea. He told people that it was only sabotage which had kept the quality of the iron's products below professional standard.

He would now demonstrate the dictatorship of the proletariat on one of the saboteurs.

One more time, Jing was taken to the scene, to suffer assault from the Revolutionary Masses. She had to bow her head down as she stood before the crowds. They shouted at her.

"Confess your crimes!"

Lee passed scissors to a Red Guard. Jing's hair had begun to grow back but now they shaved her half bald again.

Once again Jing looked like an ugly ghost. People laughed at her. But, her face was expressionless. By this time she was used to it. She just bowed her head and kept her eyes on the ground.

This kind of display was repeated, day after day until people like Lee began to want more from it. The assaults and abuses on Jing grew worse. Lee was enjoying himself and, kept thinking of new angles for his cruel game.

Then one day, Lee had an idea for a new game. First, he asked Jing to take off her work clothes during the meeting. Everyone wondered what would happen next. Then he ordered Jing to dress in her colorful clothes. Why? What would happen to her now?

The game started.

Lee ordered a Red Guard to cut holes in Jing's colorful clothes with scissors. Then, Lee grabbed her clothes, showing her skin through the holes. He spoke passionately to the crowd.

"Look! What do you see? Is there any difference between the capitalist and the Revolutionaries and Proletarians?

First, it is the skin! Capitalist's skin is whiter and more tender than ours!"

The crowd laughed.

Lee grew addicted to the game. He repeated it regularly. Jing was forced to bring her own colorful clothes with her to every assembly. If she broke the order her punishment would be even worse.

Afterwards she was always required to continue her hard labor in the furnace site. When work stopped there for the day, she still had to continue her sewing job, so Jing's working hours were longer than anyone else's.

Jing spoke to me about Lee's latest game.

"Don't tell my daughters about this one," she said.

I was unwilling to inform Sun anyway. She worried about what happened in every assembly. I just said that everything was normal, like before.

"Normal? What's normal?"

But Sun guessed something was wrong. She told me that her mother had changed. After coming home from the furnace site, Jing would shower like before, but unlike before, she no longer dressed in her colorful clothes anymore.

In fact, she seemed to hate them. Several times, she seemed about to cut the bright clothes into pieces and throw them into the fire, but always she stopped herself before taking action.

"Why is she like this?" asked Sun.

She was hoping I would tell her the true reason. But I kept my promise to Jing and did not leak the secret to her daughters.

But Jing was forced to suffer many replays of the cruel game. It must have been hard to face that crowd, knowing the abuse and assaults she would have to bear.

Every time, as the game worked up to its climax, the whole crazed crowd laughed and shouted at her, especially Lee and his son Fatty.

"Take off your clothes!"

"Take them off! Your clothes!"
"Take them off!"

And always she must obey them in the end.

But one particular day, Jing seemed different, unwilling to suffer those assaults and abuses anymore. She looked up to the sky, closing her eyes because of the strong sunshine. After a while, she opened her eyes, and looked over the heads of the crowds into some unfathomable distance.

The crowds waited.

She stood in silence but we all saw the tears that began to flow from her eyes. Her hands fluttered to her head as though she tried absently to tidy her hair. But her hands soon reminded her that she was still half bald.

The laughter and jeering of the crowd rang around her.

Suddenly, she froze into stillness.

Lee shouted at her with his cruel voice.

"Get on with it!"

The crowds mimicked his call.

"Get on with it! Get on with it!"

Looking stunned, Jing obeyed, sorting her half hair carefully, removing her dirty dark clothes, slowly dressing in her colorful clothes, managing each step with dainty fingers, checking the fastenings on her clothes and closing every button one by one, as though to ensure every detail was perfect. But this time, throughout the entire process, Jing's face remained eerily devoid of all expression.

Then, she turned and walked towards the furnace.

Lee shouted at her.

"Stop! What are you doing? Come back here!"

But this time Jing did not obey. She kept walking without the slightest pause as though she did not hear his orders. The noise of the crowd fell to a low murmur. What was Jing thinking? She walked, step by step to the furnace, and without the slightest hesitation, she threw herself into the flames.

No one had expected it. Not even Lee.

Silence fell. That silence was so sudden, so absolute, it roared.

People gaped wordlessly. Half-raised fists suddenly stopped in mid-air. Every eye was open wide, gazing in disbelief at the mouth of the furnace.

Stillness descended, as though every person in the crowd had turned to stone.

Suddenly, a movement at the edge of the crowd. Sun rushed forwards crying aloud for her mother. She ran towards the furnace. Her screams woke people up, breaking the spell. Several women ran out from the crowd and restrained her, holding her back from the furnace. But they could not stop her cries, which echoed to the sky.

This picture burned itself into our brains, never to be erased.

Meanwhile Lee was standing there maintaining an awkward silence. Then he ended his own silence by shouting aloud.

"The woman has committed suicide! She's gone to hell!"

A very few people mimicked his words but there was no passion in their voices this time. The weak response seemed to embarrass Lee.

"Everyone, go back to work!" he shouted.

There was heavy rain that night. Lightning flashed and thunder roared through all the hours of darkness. The furnace where Jing had died, collapsed during the cloud burst.

After that, a rumor spread that Jing's spirit had destroyed it. People linked it with the legend of Lady Meng Jiang, who thousands of years ago, in the Qin dynasty, had destroyed the Great Wall by crying in grief for her lost husband whom went to build the Great Wall.

Not much later, the latest guide from Chairman Mao conveyed to regions all over the country, that the local furnaces were to be given up forever. People were to be released at last from their hard and futile bondage.

My parents were so relieved to see the end of the drudgery, they praised Chairman Mao as a great leader who always made the right decision according to the circumstances of the time.

"The quality of the iron products could not match up to the professional standard!" said Father. "It was useless scrap!"

My sister interrupted, "But someone said that it was because of Jing?"

"That's only a rumor. Just focus on your bowl!"

From then on, my brother's aggression increased at the same pace as my own confusion. I became more and more confused about things that were happening daily. My brother laughed at my childishness.

First the students rebelled in schools. They called it The Students' Strike and Revolution. We did not need to go to school anymore! But this gave my brother and his classmates a need to find new ways to kill their excess time and energy.

Some of the Red Guards rushed into the temple to destroy the objects inside. They called their action "Destroy Four Olds". These were "Old Customs, Old Culture, Old Habits, and Old Ideas". They said that "Olds" should be destroyed, in order to build a "New" world.

So they smashed the altar and desks and chairs, burning out the ancestral woodcarvings, shouting aloud at the monks, pasting Revolutionary Slogans on the walls.

"Down with bad elements!"

"Down with imperialism!"

"Down with foreign religion!"

"Down with the Christians!"

"Down with the counter revolutionists!"

The monks tried hard to protect their belongings, but they failed. The Red Guards whipped them with belts until the monks fell to the ground covered with blood.

The monks exhorted the violent youths.

"How dare you! Who are you to abuse the Buddha?"

"We are the Red Guards of Chairman Mao! We are not afraid of your ghosts!"

"They are only statues of the Buddha!"

"That is exactly what we want to destroy!"

"You will get retribution one day!"

My Grandpa passed by chance as it was happening. He tried to stop the Red Guards destroying the Buddha statues.

"What is this bullshit?" said Grandpa, "What are you doing?"

"We destroy the 'Four Olds' to establish 'New Customs, New Culture, New Habits, and New Ideas'!"

Grandpa shouted at them.

"You are crazy creatures!"

The Red Guards retaliated by attacking Grandpa. My brother argued with the other Red Guards and fought back.

My brother came home with a bloody nose. He explained what had happened, but Father did not care what reason he had. He gave my brother a good beating.

"I told you to keep out of trouble! Don't do it again."

My brother was frustrated not to be able to escape Father's authority to do as he pleased in the world. But later, his chance came. Chairman Mao called for the "Educated Youth" of the nation to go and learn the farming life and reform themselves away from the comforts of towns.

My brother took the initiative and went to a country village, to work full time and learn alongside real farmers. Before leaving, he raised up his fist to salute the portrait of Chairman Mao on the wall.

"We will follow Chairman Mao forever!"

Then he left home for his new life.

Later, he wrote to complain about how tough it was living and working in the countryside.

My parents got the letter from him, but could do nothing about it, except encourage him.

"Hold on, for the sake of the family!"

We mailed some food to him, but occasionally, he escaped back home, just for a good dinner.

Sometimes I missed my brother and took the comic book out from its secret hiding place. I wanted to read it, but could not. Before he left, he'd told me that the strange language in the book was English.

But even though I could not read it, just holding the book evoked memories; summer, swimming, fishing, fishing gear...Ahn... so many pictures that blurred together in my brain.

Chapter 33

Time passed.

Years later, the unthinkable happened. Chairman Mao died. By that time, we were receiving news via radio broadcasts and newspapers, but still people could not believe it at first. Could this be a rumor made by the enemy? Somehow, we had all believed that our great leader Chairman Mao would live forever.

But, when the news was confirmed, everyone seemed to panic. All over China people thought that without him they must lose all purpose and direction.

After accepting the truth at last, the town arranged a memorial service for Chairman Mao, to be held in the school campus. The crowds cried for him and blocked the campus with wreaths. There were thousands of white paper flowers and so much heartbroken crying, it was hard to believe.

"Why did you leave us?"

"We can't live without you!"

But after his death, the speed of change increased, the most important being Economic Reform. China's doors began to open to the outside world.

Little by little, day after day, Chinese lives normalized. Educational qualifications became more and more important. I started learning English and studied hard because I wanted to control my own fate.

After graduating from university, I got a chance to continue my studies abroad and met up with Sun in the United States of America at last. It was an amazing moment for both of us. Neither of us had ever expected to meet again in our lifetimes.

Sun told me that she had been living in America for years. After her mother's death, her overseas relatives did all they could to move her and Star out of China to begin life in the USA.

The first time we met, I brought the comic book named Snow White and The Seven Dwarfs to show to her. Sun seemed visibly moved at the sight of it, for a moment I thought she might burst into tears, but she controlled herself, and asked where I had got it.

I told her how my brother had procured it for me all those years ago. I had never spilled the secret to her at the time. Sun asked after my brother. I told her that he had lived in a countryside village for more than ten years.

"Change came too late for him. His life was already spoiled. He returned home to us at last, but could never find work in our town. He had to go to the big city to look for chances. But, it was difficult for him, because of his educational background and age. He can only do physical labor."

Sun listened to my story and was silent for a while.

Then, we began talking over the memories from our shared past, but not all our memories were sad, we remembered the good times too.

Sun was now a qualified psychologist, but she had chosen to work as a fashion designer. She showed me some of her designs. The clothes she created were as full of colour and style as anyone could wish. I was happy for her.

Sun explained that originally her family had moved back to China from a tropical country where the culture was so light-hearted and relaxed that everyone wore colorful clothes.

"We dressed like tropical butterflies. The colors made us all feel happy and hopeful."

I surprised her by saying that my own mother could sew clothes now.

"She went to great effort to learn because there were no tailors in our town after your family were gone. Residents missed your mother's skills very much."

Suddenly, I wanted to figure out a mystery. At the time of Jing's death, her daughters were forbidden to be at the furnace site. How was it that Sun had appeared there at the very moment of Jing's death?

"What made you come to the scene that day?"

Sun was thoughtful for a time. She seemed to be combing her memory seeking the relevant details she needed to solve the mystery.

"It was Star. I remember now. Star got suddenly sick. I was worried she might have a serious illness. I went to try to persuade Mother to come home and help her."

Tears began to flow over Sun's face.

"It was the last time I saw my mother alive."

When she calmed at last, Sun asked me how the small town was doing now? She had lived there for years and was curious about the place that held so many memories for her.

I told her the town had been destroyed by a great flood years ago.

"It was almost completely washed away."

Sun sighed and lapsed into silence.

I knew there must be many questions in her mind, questions about people and memories that she preferred not to touch upon. So we steered our conversation away from the past and began to discuss our new lives and futures.

But that shared past will live within us always, whether we speak of it or not.

End

Acknowledgement

Many thanks to a number of people for helping me in my English writing and publishing, especially my wife, Sophia; my editors, Tui Allen (this book's editor), Ray Hecht; my excellent translators, Jicheng Sun, Hal Swindall, Xiaowen Yang and Yan Ding; critics Ruicai Kong; reviewer Hilton Yip; my most excellent readers, Emilia Tagaza, Jenny Chin; and my great publisher, Whyte Tracks publishing.

- Xie Hong

About the Author

Xie Hong is an award-winning author, novelist and poet, based in China. He was born in Canton and graduated from East China Normal University, Shanghai, with an economics degree, then studied English at the Waikato Institute of Technology in New Zealand. He began writing poetry in 1985, but turned his attention to fiction in 1993. He has authored 14 books and his short stories have appeared in *World Literature Today, Pathlight,* and *Renditions.* Currently, he lives in mainland China.

'Mao's Town' is book one of the forth-coming trilogy entitled *'Mao's Children'* which is set in the historically important Mao ZeDong era.

Published

Whyte Tracks publishing
Stengade 51 D
3000 Helsingør
Denmark
www.whytetracsk-publishing.com